THE RÉSERVATION

BY
LOU GLOVER

First edition 2023

Acknowledgements
Thank you to my boys…both big and small.
To my family & friends for always having my back.
And to Jan and Jo for believing that I can.

CHAPTER 1

Then...
KATE

Thursday

I hit the privacy setting.

The location service on my phone has remained resolutely off since the first night I met him. Still...I check it again in case Tom for any mad reason is sat at home, tracking my whereabouts. My red pin could be weaving and dirty dancing its way across east London, not Brighton, where his lying tart of a wife said she would be.

I had kept things vague and casual sounding over breakfast, reminding Tom that Jules and I were hosting one of our 'pink pig' champagne & charcuterie events tonight in Brighton and would therefore be doing an overnighter.

Our monthly 'Pink Pig' pop up restaurant was in hot demand ever since our feature in the Evening Standard. It was a simple concept that Jules and I had hit on drunkenly and wrote on a fag packet a few years ago along with hundreds of other pissed, discarded ideas on how to make our millions …except this one had stuck.

We imported unusual, spiced meats and cheese, paired them with figs, walnuts, honey and cranberries and served with the most delicious sparkling wine and champagne from around the continent. There was no kitchen required or trained chef needed …it was simple and delicious. Rustic trestle tables were set up in various locations and draped with hand crocheted white tablecloths that we bought from local car boot sales and then decorated with huge gothic candelabras. The low spend- high margin afforded us a variety of eclectic jazz musicians and buskers to ensure that each night felt unique.

The article in the Standard (although glowing) had referred to Jules, myself and our assistant Mary as, 'The three little pigs' which Mary and I found highly amusing, but Jules was livid having gone up two dress sizes since we began importing cheese.

I had waved my hand towards the battered family calendar this morning …as actual proof of tonight's event. Our calendar had frankly seen better days and was looking grubbier and more full of lies than its owner as it hung precariously from the wall with a loose drawing pin.

My palms had felt clammy …but much to my shame, there was that revolting little thrill in my tummy at the possibility of being caught.

A part of me wanted Tom to find out, wanted to punish and hurt us both. We didn't deserve to be happy. How could we be happy when our little girl was dead.

"It was a terrible accident" the policewoman had explained gently that day, as if somehow that made it more palatable. Connie had only been a few steps ahead of Tom on her new scooter and the shriek of metal was heard all the way into the village.

Neighbours, shopkeepers and random strangers all ran to help, one of them holding Tom in her arms until the ambulance arrived but there was nothing anyone could do. Connie had just pressed her back break a little too late. Simple as that.

The driver was eighty-four without so much as a parking ticket in over sixty years of driving, but it wasn't enough to stop him ploughing into our little girl. He was inconsolable.

Tom admitted immediately to the policewoman that he had taken his eyes off Connie just for a few minutes whilst replying to a work email. He hadn't been able to look at me as he told her, and we never spoke of it …

then or since. The policewoman assured him that he still wouldn't have been able to stop her, and Tom grabbed gratefully onto this pardon like it were a life jacket out in the Atlantic. He felt comforted if not exonerated by her words, but her words did nothing for me and a small seed of hate for him planted into my womb, exactly where I had carried her.

Shock and untold grief had eventually morphed into indifference over the last four year. There was a method in my madness …if I didn't give a fuck about anything then nothing else could hurt that bad again could it. No more danger.

But a careless and indifferent woman is really the most dangerous of all.

Freddie was now our only child and not out of choice or as nature intended but because of the worst kind of horror.

He kept Tom and I together despite the growing resentment. He should have been enough to keep me from spiralling out of control but while I was still able to shower Fred with the love I had left, I also showered my self loathing and anger in a hotel room…with him. Dominic Box.

As I near our hotel, I cross just up by the traffic lights and opposite the East Green, sticking to the busy hustle of Shoreditch high street. Some weeks I've risked a short cut to The Huxley Hotel via the slightly dodgy looking park, praying not to be mugged at knifepoint as I dart past the swings with crotch less knickers and a sensible coat but tonight, I stick to the main road.

"Kate" his voice sounds gruff and his breath tingles inside my ear as he jogs close behind me and up the large stone steps of the Huxley Hotel.

Dominic Box isn't what you would call a beautiful man …he's tall with black hair, piercing blue eyes and cocky Irish charm …tick, tick, tick …but his nose is broken and slightly too big for his face and his permanent scowl is intimidating at best, terrifying at worst.

If anything, he looks a bit of an arsehole …which as we know, is strangely appealing to lots of women.

It's highly possible that he is in fact a complete arsehole, but I don't need to dig that deep, I just need a quick fix to take me away from my own head and thoughts.

He stares at me and even in the dark it's clear to see that we are as different physically as night and day.

My light olive skin looks even darker set against his pale Irish skin and his hair is as black as coal next to my white blonde.

"Are you hungry?" He holds my chin a little roughly.

"We can grab a drink …or go straight up to the room?" He gives a lazy wink and smirks.

"Your room" I say.

He's silent but doesn't break eye contact as we take the lift up to the room.

I stare back… boldly, my body burning up already like I'm coming down with the flu.

He moves in close, and I think he's about to kiss me but instead he grabs the nape of my neck with his left hand, staring hard as he yanks down my tights roughly with the other.

Sliding his hand expertly down my knickers, I hold my breath.

Inwardly I curse at wearing tights…unsexy as hell. I had planned to get rid of them before he arrived. He couldn't care less about my tights and bending his knees slightly he lets his fingers dip softly inside.

My mind clears and immediately I'm free from this never-ending emptiness, free from the persistent pain in my chest. Free.

I'm reach up to kiss him with my tongue, but he pulls back.

"No." He says firmly.

"I want to look at your face as you cum".

And I do

"Ahhh fuck, I forgot the hotel key card" he says as I smooth my dress back down.

We head back down to the foyer and Dominic saunters boldly over to the desk.

"Mr & Mrs Box" he says smoothly to the Receptionist.

"Our usual Reservation".

JASON

"Here we go?" Jason chortled, sitting back in his chair in the basement of the hotel. Pushing his lank fringe back into his ponytail, he moved in for a closer look across the multiple screens. The hotel security cameras covered every inch of The Huxley apart from the bedrooms… more's the pity.

He clicked on camera thirteen ... narrowing his eyes. The grainy lift zoomed into sight as Jason leaned back and watched the tall guy in the grey coat pull her tights back up.

She re-fastened the belt on her coat, flicking her long, blonde hair over one shoulder. Over and over, she tied her belt as Jason hit rewind and play.

You didn't see women as hot as that every day of the week, that was for sure. She had that beach babe look about her, lightly tanned with very pale blonde hair and a cracking figure on her. Jason reached down and unbuckled his own thick belt with a groan.

The pair of them had been coming to the hotel every Thursday for the last year or so. The dark-haired bloke regularly swanned into the lobby with his expensive clothes and smug face.

He looked Irish… and despite his cash, he still looked a bit rough. Maybe it was the squashed nose or the moody look he always had on his mush, but he looked like someone who had seen a few scrapes over the years.

Jason made it his business to find out the names of all the regulars at the hotel and anyone who just happened to catch his eye. Dominic Box particularly irritated him, the arrogant fuck, swanning around, paying with cash, and ordering champagne like it was water.

The two of them always stayed in the most expensive room, The Duke of Shoreditch, which was the only suite in the hotel and had a luxurious glass bath… more of a tank, really.

Jason coughed angrily, rolled back his stale tongue, and hurled the phlegm as hard as he could at the screen. It hit Dominic Box square in the face. He laughed before rubbing down the screen with his blue sleeve.

"Loaded twat".

CHAPTER 2

DOMINIC

Thursday

"Ok, Hels, give the kids a kiss from me. I'll see you tomorrow night."

I toss my mobile back onto the king-sized bed.

I didn't want to lie to Helena, but I had no choice really …nothing I did pleased her, so it was partly her own fault.

She was only forty-four, too young to be menopausal, surely… although the thought *had* crossed my mind.

I heard some women went nuts once their ovaries logged off, and she was definitely becoming more irrational every month, complaining constantly and never believing where I was and what I was doing… It was unbearable.

Her permanent, hard face did nothing to harden anything below for me, and that was the other elephant in the room.

Helena insisted it must be a physical problem (with me), nagging me to get my prostrate checked. Who checks their prostrate at forty-five? When that came back all clear, she moved on to my mental health. It must be psychological… I must be depressed or stressed or both, that's why I couldn't get it up…so I agreed to see a therapist for six sessions to shut her up.

It didn't enter her mind for a second that it might be her own doing…her nagging and moaning and complaining, hardly an aphrodisiac for any man. I didn't want to be with her anymore, but I also didn't want to end up with half my money and the kids hating me, either. For now, Kate was the best solution to that conundrum.

My wife paraded us as the perfect family to anyone who would listen. The gluten-free dinner parties, the swanky health club membership that cost a small mortgage. Her Instagram friends liking her album of bullshit with endless fake comments.

The famous five, we beamed out of the grid week after week… living the dream. It made my stomach churn…meanwhile, muggings paid for it all. She was deluded, and I had no patience with it.

She looked after the kids well enough …with a little help from our pretty (but not too pretty) au pair, but she had become lazy, with no opinions of her own and endless moaning about where I was and who I was with day and night. She smelt my disinterest like a narcotics dog, and the lack of physical interaction from me only fueled her resentment further, which turned me off even more.

Helena filled our sexual void with endless gym workouts. Her body was as hard as her face, and I filled the gap with meaningless one-night stands to tide me over…although now I had Kate, it was actually more convenient… one regular woman on the side made sense while work was so busy. Kate was aloof too, which I liked; she didn't question me and had me working for her attention which kept things interesting…so interesting that before I knew it, we were over a year in.

I had grabbed a quick beer with James, one of the dads from my son's school, before heading to The Huxley for our weekly hook-up.

James only wanted the physical details, not the emotional…good lad.

Was she good in bed? Did she have any hot mates? Did she take it up the arse? I laughed at his predictability, but his gleaming eyes did make me a bit uneasy, to be honest. My rule of thumb is to keep what I'm doing and who I'm doing it with to myself…no sharing with mates, no sharing with Kate and certainly no sharing with Helena. Better to be off-grid as much as possible in my experience… as people thought they wanted to hear the truth but rarely liked it. I had mentioned her to James, though, after he spotted Kate and I leaving the hotel one morning.

"Hey…don't mention any of this to Nicole," I remind him again, like a broken record… but I had that horrible feeling that he was one of those dick heads that told their Mrs. everything.

"Mate! That goes without saying. What goes on tour." He punches my arm twice.

"We're in Liverpool Street, Jim… hardly on tour."

He had given a leery wink and a smirk as we laughed into our pint glasses.

Still… something about the conversation reminded me of an old saying of my Mother's, "Loose lips sink ships, Dominic."

I drained my pint and ordered an Uber.

I always book the same room for us at The Huxley. The Duke of Shoreditch is the only *suite* in the hotel and sits generously across the corner of the third floor, with clear views of both the East Green Park and Shoreditch high street. Its biggest pull was the gigantic bath that sat in front of the floor-length windows. Nicknamed 'The Tank' by staff and guests, it was clear glass, and you could swim from one side to another; it was that big. Watching Kate sculling naked through the clear glass was worth every extra penny they charged for the room.

I've only ever brought Kate here; none of the others have been treated this well.

My phone beeps again from the bed… it's her.

"Just got to the tube, be with you in ten. K."

I grab my coat and phone, hunting for the key card but can't find it... fuck it, I decide to head back down and meet her. I'm too wired to wait.

I see her before she sees me. She looks gorgeous and carefree… though I know she's anything but…but I can't fix her baggage or anyone else's, not even my own, so I don't get into any of that with her. We're here for a good time only. If she wants to talk or, god forbid, cry, she's got a therapist for that, which ironically is where we met. Therapy was not my thing, but it got Helena to quieten down the nagging for a while. On a good note, the therapist did lead me to Kate, though.

She fiddles with her long, blonde hair nervously. I like that she's nervous.

I wonder if Tom even slightly suspects his wife of having an affair.

I wonder how pissed off she would be if she knew I had met him already. The thought makes me smirk.

"Kate", I breathe into her ear…

CHAPTER 3

TEDDY

Friday

I've arrived nice and early at The Huxley. I need a quick leveller before I see Amanda again and Rico, the head barman fixed me the perfect gin and tonic. I tip my glass towards him with a grin.

"Spot on Rico… lovely", I call to him.

"Pleasure Mr Villandry; I'll grab you some olives," he disappears around to the other side of the large, deeply set, oval bar.

You would think meeting Amanda twice a week, I'd be pretty relaxed by the whole thing now, four months in…four months in… but nope, I feel as shifty as I did on the first night I booked her. I'm small town… a suburban fella. Sleeping with an escort is not very 'me'. I'm not *that* bloke.

I've enjoyed my share of strip clubs over the years for sure…the usual… clients, stag do's. But I had never, ever paid for sex … not until Suzie left me.

Amanda (my escort) chose the Huxley about a month after we met. I'm not entirely sure what was wrong with our original hotel over in Covent Garden, but for some reason, she wanted to try The Huxley, and I have to say, I was impressed from the off. It's a hidden gem, fairly unknown.

Amanda badgered me into booking the most expensive room here, The Duke of Shoreditch. The Duke is the only suite in the hotel with the most incredible huge bath that resembles a glass fish tank.

She hadn't seemed overly impressed on our first visit, perhaps not as fancy as she expected or is used to… but she insisted we stick with it all the same.

The Huxley is exactly to my taste. That perfect blend of old-school glamour and modern, effortless charm. Homely. I was pleasantly surprised to find none of the usual wankiness here that many of the Shoreditch hotels flaunt these days.

The building was previously part of the old Midland bank and had those gloriously high ceilings throughout, with a stunning staircase that fanned gracefully across the lobby. The gaping mouth of the staircase was guarded by two lanterns, which sat like proud lions on either side of the bannister. The effect was intimate and, dare I say, romantic… which certainly helped gloss over the salubrious nature of my visits.

Divorce is right up there as one of the top three most stressful events, and whoever wrote that list sure as shit wasn't exaggerating.

I take a large slurp of my Hendricks and accept the dish of chilli and lemon olives that Rico places in front of me.

My own divorce had felt like a slow and very painful death with no farewell party or piss-up to soften the blow. I had kissed goodbye to my past and all my hopes for our future with just one shitty letter from Suzie's solicitor. Paula Dean, 'The Reigate Rottweiler'.

I was out on my ear, just like that… and within months, some other arsehole was sitting eating his cereal with *my* kids every morning. Breaking bread and hearts at *my* fucking table. The table *I* bought for her when she insisted she preferred this one to the cheaper, identical one over at Ikea.

"Why us and not them? Tell me that, Suzie?" I had ranted when she first asked me to leave. Why had the shitty, boring couple at number nineteen, with sweet F.A. in common and not a good word to say about each other, stayed married for thirty years? Yet the two of us, who loved *and* liked each other, which was something these days…failed so miserably. It still made no sense fourteen months later.

My life capsized with a friendly shove from that butch, nasty bitch, Paula Dean. Man, overboard, and that man was me. It was cruel. I had absolutely no control over anything anymore.

My work was suffering; I couldn't sleep, I couldn't concentrate, and I had started to make stupid mistakes. It was only a matter of time before I was caught and my boss found out what I had been doing. I was in way over my head, borrowing from Peter to pay for Paul. Paul and his three greedy, fat mates.

When Charles took me for an unscheduled lunch at The Dean Street Townhouse a few weeks ago, I felt sure I was about to get the bullet. I had misjudged the old bastard, though, and instead, he said he liked me. 'One of life's good guys' was the expression he used. He wanted to help.

Charles, a divorcee himself, knew it was horrific and couldn't have been nicer. It made me feel even more wretched about having my fingers in the till.

Charles reminded me that Delaney & Kilbride offer six free counselling sessions per year for all employees as well as their Friday fruit basket, pension plan and Bupa.

"All the big Corp companies are doing it now, Ted. Buying into this mindful bollocks".

I did as he suggested and listened, agitated as the counsellor explained that my main issue was not being present or grateful in life. Whaaaaat?

Grateful for what, woman? My poky bedsit? My halved pension? My wife's new arsehole? (HIM) I mean… her new fella, not her actual… anyway…

The counsellor suggested meditating at home… whilst burning her patented frankincense sticks, which she peddled at the end of each 'free' session. (£36 for a pack of five). Mindful moonlighting.

Human contact is key to my recovery, apparently and as a natural people pleaser, I burn her sticks obediently in my hotel room right before I screw my escort. This pleases me much more than the sticks themselves, but it ticks the "human contact" box. Two birds… one stick.

She's a good girl, my escort. Amanda is far too posh and educated to be working as such, which makes me feel mildly better about the whole thing.

She seems … I don't know. Cleaner somehow, and I don't mean 'downstairs'… just generally, cleaner. A good girl.

"Same again, Rico" I raise my empty glass and give it a cursory shake. "Make it a large one, and could you send this one to my room, please, 'The Duke of Shoreditch."

JASON

"Ted Villandry's in again", Jason smirked as Steve arrived, joining him on tonight's shift. He hovered his mouse over the screen that covered the hotel foyer.

Ted Villandry had salesman written all over him. The easy chat with the bar staff, the confident swagger and the twice weekly bedroom habits with that posh whore.

Travelling salesmen loved an escort; everyone knew that. Except this sleaze wasn't a salesman, he worked for some kind of bank.

A few weeks back, he had left his Jacket behind on one of his many visits. It wound up in security and lost property. Jason had rifled through for any loose notes, but the tight wad was carrying no cash, just a few business cards.

A quick Google of Teddy Villandry at 'Delaney & Kilbride' had revealed him as the Client Director for an investment brokerage, whatever that was. Boring fuck.

Jason zoomed in on him now, sat on a barstool, guzzling gin…

The bar looked pretty quiet tonight, apart from a couple of regulars and a group of after-work drinkers.

Everyone in here generally irritated the crap out of Jason. Loaded, spoilt, chubby Tories, all of them. He was particularly irritated by the ones that could afford the posh suite here, week after week. Jason knew exactly how much they charged for The Duke of Shoreditch, and it was enough to make your eyes water, more than he earned in an entire week.

Made his blood boil.

CHAPTER 4

AMANDA

Friday

The whole world was having meaningless sex on Tinder, Hinge, Raya, and God knows where else; I wasn't any worse than your average woman on a dating app… just because I accepted a little financial help, it didn't make me a bad person.

Teddy was one of my favourites. Brimming with charisma, kind, funny, attractive and, more importantly, a very generous tipper. I'd been seeing him twice a week now for about four months.

He spent more time chatting than doing anything else. He was lonely. He missed his wife, that was clear, and it suited me just fine, keeping him company; I felt lonely too. His money was paying for my reflexology course at Kings College and half of my rent, so we were both happy with the transaction.

The Huxley Hotel, although my suggestion, was a bit too quirky for my tastes, but I had my reasons for needing to be there and in *that* suite.

Luckily Teddy loved the place and was happy to keep booking it. He loved the old gramophone that sat grandly in the corner of the bar...crooning Etta James and Frank Sinatra. The old-fashioned décor and ambience were quite a stark contrast to the cool, bearded hipsters who filled the restaurant and bar downstairs each week. They slugged on margaritas and flirted with anyone who had a pulse, before hopping on a Boris bike to make up for their seven flights per month. Teddy was different…not a hint of pretentious; he was an old-school gent despite being only forty-three.

Tonight, as I arrived, the house manager, Joseph, greeted me as always, like an important guest. Waving his hands dramatically to the left with an imaginary red carpet as he gallantly hailed the lift for me …like I were Dame Judi Dench and not (as we both knew) a very expensive escort.

They say money talks, but honestly, I found it was the opposite. Nine times out of ten, money kept mouths politely closed.

As I strode from the lift, I reached for my phone at the bottom of my bag. My skin prickled as I read the message.

WhatsApp

"Is your phone broken, Mandy? I can always collect my money in person. The Huxley Hotel… right?"

Oh, God. Why wouldn't he leave me alone?

My old dealer, Jimmy Billington.

JASON

Something caught Jason's eye on screen six…hmmm… that tart arriving in reception to meet Ted Villandry again.

The first time he had seen her, he mistook her for the other blonde bird that stayed with Dominic Box. On closer inspection, he realised this girl was a few years younger, a bit skinnier and not quite as pretty… too much slap on her face, but both had that just been shagged, messy blonde hair that caught most eyes.

She was fairly tall and slim with green, cat-shaped eyes and smooth, olive skin. She turned most heads in here and probably made a fortune from these lonely idiots. He doubted many of the guests suspected she was a prostitute. She certainly didn't dress like a tart, often turned up in jeans and a t-shirt under her expensive coat… but he had seen her counting her money in the lift on her way down. He knew exactly what she was.

His mum always said how manipulative girls could be and regularly warned him to stay away from the slutty girls on their old council estate in Putney. There really hadn't been much need as his angry face and wiry frame acted as some kind of woman repeller anyway.

Her blonde hair bounces on the screen in front of him, like she's advertising some fancy shampoo.

He watches with irritation as Joseph hails the lift. The sycophant looked like he might even courtesy to her. She smiles brightly at him, used to this level of attention, then disappears into the lift and up to meet Ted Villandry.

Jason clicked onto the camera inside the lift and ran his finger across the screen, left to right, just where her breasts must be, tucked under her leather jacket. He wished to God he could get a camera inside those bedrooms. He was getting pretty bored and pissed off, only catching the trailers. There must be a better way.

CHAPTER 5

KATE

Thursday

I straighten my dress as the lift door opens and follow him down the familiar corridor to our hotel suite. Pain and excitement etched tightly across my brow as I followed him down the corridor of the hotel.

Dominic had appeared unexpectedly in the private waiting room that random afternoon.

I'd been seeing the grief counsellor, Susan Steinberg, twice a week since we lost Connie.

Our mothers had staged some kind of intervention, driving me there each week, not trusting me to leave my bed or black hole if left to my own devices.

I didn't have the strength to argue. I no longer cared about anything by then, other than Freddie, of course.

Freddie was the only thing that kept me vaguely on the rails. Just long enough to kiss him goodbye each morning at the school gate, long enough to remember to pack his P.E kit and long enough to wipe away his tears as he cried each morning for his big sister.

I told him again and again that Connie was watching us from a big marshmallow cloud, probably still doing backflips and her impressive splits, even up in the sky. Freddie would rub his pink, squinty eyes and give me a brave, big boy smile before Miss March gently extracted him from me… taking his damp, little hand gently into her own and patting my arm ever so lightly. Those little acts of kindness were always the things that moved me the most. The touch of an arm, the squeeze of a hand from a stranger. Human touch kept me alive.

Two years on, and the tears and grief iced over into a numb nothing. The brain's clever way of managing trauma. My heart felt still, my eyes were blank, and my voice was slow… but at least I functioned without crying or without our mothers on tap.

I began working again, scaling up 'The Pink Pig' from the security of our home. Another year passed, and the business began to grow, and I threw myself into work with Jules holding my hand. Tom and I took our first holiday just with Freddie, we saw old friends again, we even laughed…. but inside, I felt nothing.

I performed well on the surface so as not to cause our families more concern. My public pain fueled their own. Everyone felt better if I at least 'appeared' sane.

Tom and I dealt with our gut-wrenching grief in a Mars versus Venus kind of way, a united front on the outside but dying a different death on the in.

Tom wanted us all to thrive, not survive; I wanted to scream at him daily and ask him how the fuck he could have taken his eye off her even for a second, how he could live with himself, how could he be the tiniest bit happy. Instead, I stayed silent; if I opened that box, I would never stop, and our family would be completely broken.

The silence and pretence of forgiveness, along with the grief that drowned me from the inside out, made me want to go crazy. If it hadn't been for Freddie, I'd have been more blatant, but instead, I saved my madness for just after his bedtime. I wanted to do everything you aren't supposed to… because why not? Why toe the line and be a good person when life blew up in your face anyway?

Secretly I drank most days, then I would smile calmly and prepare dinner from scratch. A nutritious dinner for our diminished family as the silent tumour of resentment grew bigger inside my gut.

As I waited that day for Dr Steinberg to call my name, blankly thumbing through an old magazine, I felt someone standing over me.

There he was. Dominic Box. Unsmiling, silent… moody… but for the first time in the longest time, I had felt the faintest flicker of something I couldn't even remember.

"You're sat on my coat", he had said.

He stared hard into my eyes for longer than necessary… but still no smile came to his thick lips. He looked pissed off, if anything.

I reached for his grey overcoat and held it out to him, neither speaking nor smiling myself, yet holding his stare defiantly.

We seemed to look at one another for an uncomfortable amount of time, but it could only have been seconds before a muffled sound interrupted this moment… whatever it was.

"Mrs Golding…. MRS GOLDING? Ms Steinberg will see you now."

Hastily I stood up, but unusually he hadn't bothered to step back and allow me any space, and so our bodies had touched by accident…or perhaps not. My eyes were level with his shoulders; I didn't look up again at that intimidating face, so we stood still and close.

"Mrs Golding", he murmured slowly. I looked up in surprise, and he smiled lazily. Then he was gone.

As I follow him now to the Duke of Shoreditch Suite, I still feel the same thrill. Sometimes escape was the only way to survive the living hell.

The Huxley suite is in darkness… but before I can negate the lighting, he pushes me back against the door, taking my face firmly in his large hands as he lets his warm, thick tongue find mine. He turns me around, pressing my cheek to the cold door as he lifts my coat and dress up with one hand and yanks my tights and knickers down with the other. I am breathing short, shallow breaths now, my hands raised and flat against the room door as he moves in. I am ready. He enters me roughly from behind with ease. We move in sync as if our bodies were made to fit together perfectly, as if we have known each other for a lifetime. His energy and heat always take me by surprise, and his wanting is such a huge turn-on. I feel no inhibition as I grind aggressively, hungry… angry. I twist my neck towards him, needing to feel his tongue on mine. The urgency of our tongues, like two wild dogs and the sensation of my plump mouth over his tips him over the edge first before I meet him a fraction of a second later. We heave against the door, his deep moan drowning out my own.

Afterwards, we slide to the floor and sit side-by-side, silent but for our heavy breath. My shoes and coat are still on, and my tights are tangled with my knickers and twisted around my ankles. I look over to him, and finally, he smiles, reaching over to brush the damp hair gently back from my cheek... his eyes never leave mine. The guilt only kicks in once we are done… and already I have the urge to go home to what's left of my family.

My phone flashes from the top of my bag, and even from over here, I know that it is Tom.

CHAPTER 6

DOMINIC

Thursday

I rubbed the shampoo roughly into my scalp.

Of course, Tom was calling her, wanting to know where she was. If I were him, I wouldn't let her out of my sight. I was getting sick of sharing her and answering to him all the time.

Weirdly, I hadn't felt as much guilt as I should when I first started to pick up the occasional one-nighter.

Like a man needs food and water, he needs sex, and that's all it was on each occasion. A pretty woman in a bar, a temp at work, the sister of a mate…they had all been fun but forgettable and allowed me to carry on as normal at home for the sake of the kids.

I tried everything to help Helena feel better… suggested she loose a few pounds and get her confidence back… even paid for a fancy gym for her, but she still complained. I told her to book an appointment with her GP to discuss upping her anti-depressants. I tried all I could, but nothing changed. It had become tedious.

In the meantime, I felt like the occasional game of squash with a different player was nothing major and would prevent things from imploding completely at home.

Women. I loved them but fuck me… they were hard work.

In the end, I agreed to six therapy sessions to quieten down her paranoia.

Dr Steinberg had proved to be surprisingly helpful in more ways than one. Despite the uncomfortable bleating on about my feelings and childhood… which was exhausting and self-indulgent, it was Dr Steinberg who led me to Kate.

I saw her in the waiting room around twelve months ago, lost in some trashy magazine, but occasionally she bit nervously on her thumb and something about the way she moved felt so familiar. She was hot; there was no doubt about that. The guys would call her a milf for sure with her thick, wavy, blonde hair, soft green eyes, elongated nose and full lips, but it was something else… an air about her, an aura, I don't know.

I wanted to go straight over to her, and luckily for me, she was sitting on the edge of my coat. I hadn't realized I had left it out here, but sure enough, the sleeve was caught underneath her ass. I suppressed a smile at the basic thought of her ass (simple creatures) and moved towards her. I can still picture her face… the first time she looked up at me. I couldn't take my eyes off her. She was weirdly familiar, and yet I couldn't place her or figure out who it was that she reminded me of.

I can't blame Tom for checking up on her now. I would do the same if she were mine, but it pisses me off.

"Room for two in there" she pulls her jumper dress over her head and throws her bra onto the tiles, climbing into the shower beside me. The remote control sets off, and my hard-on springs back into action at the sight of her naked. I forget Tom and my moaning, paranoid wife.

CHAPTER 7

TEDDY

Friday

I'm nursing my third gin as I lay back on the king-sized bed in the suite.

Shoes and jacket strewn on the floor, and feeling mildly but nicely pissed as I work my way through endless emails.

The expense from this weekly room service was nuts, not to mention the lip service for Amanda herself. My head throbs slightly as I glance at each astronomical figure glaring back from my screen. I eyeball each online statement in fresh horror. I promised myself I wouldn't touch anyone else's account at work, but I'm falling deeper and deeper into the shit as the days go by.

I hadn't wanted to split with Suzie; it was her choice… and although catastrophic, I understood why. I had been absent for most of our marriage. As faithful and loyal as our labrador, Pablo… but absent all the same... I loved her completely… still did… but I'd neglected her badly and was having to pay the heaviest price. I'd lived and breathed this damn company, couldn't think about anything else, and now even my career was about to be ruined as well.

Over the years, I convinced myself I was doing it all for "us"… for our family, for a better life, but if truth be told, I loved what I was doing; I didn't want to delegate, to leave the office or the party early. I didn't want a more ambitious colleague taking my clients to the best restaurant… closing my deals. It became all-consuming. My mornings became earlier, my evenings became later, and my holidays became shorter. Suzie complained, then cried, then complained some more, but all the while, I kept my foot on the gas and my eye on the prize…partnership into the firm and a guaranteed healthy profit share, which would set us up for life. All it did was drive her further and further away until eventually, and without me even noticing, she stopped nagging or, more importantly, caring. It turns out that when the nagging stops, you're fucked.

We kept things amicable for the kids, but inside I felt destroyed the day she asked me to leave our home.

Alone in a poxy flat, with the kids every other weekend and the deafening silence that fell in-between their sulky visits, I was aching with loneliness. I couldn't face dating, all these modern apps asking you to swipe left and right or the modern way…sending a dick pic. It was new and baffling to me, and frankly, booking an escort had seemed the less seedy route. It was the most logical and practical solution for a quick burst of female company.

They sent Amanda to me on that first night, four months ago… and as a creature of habit, I haven't ever thought to ask for anyone else since. I've grown fond of her as she's my main source of company these days, and I feel pretty at ease with her. I like to think she genuinely likes me and not just my cash. Naïve? Hopeful? Possibly both. She never judges, and right now, that's what I need.

"Teddy, even nice men book girls like me…you would be surprised? I don't care what you do or where you do it." She had soothed when I told her my life was snowballing.

Amanda was a good girl; if you forgot she was an escort, which I conveniently had. She barely drank, let alone anything else. An occasional cigarette was her one and only vice, and not any old cigarette but one of those super slim, fancy white ones. Vogue, I think she called them or something pretentious. She could be bossy and sassy for sure, but underneath, there was a real vulnerability about her that made me want to take care of her.

I drain my gin and then open the wine, pouring myself a large glass. Unlike her, I do very much like a drink. I gulp back half a glass before answering her silly coded knock on the room door.

"Hello, Teddy", she purrs in her sexy, posh husk.

Amanda has the look of "Good stock". Tall, athletic with thick, long blonde hair and green eyes. The poster girl for health and vitality. To look at her in her expensive, fashionable clothes, you might assume she worked in fashion or perhaps in sales, which I suppose she does in her own sweet way.

She kisses me on each cheek as if we are dear friends, before confidently kicking off her heels and undressing with abandon. Naked, she chatters away, asking me polite and interesting questions about my day as she pours herself a San Pellegrino and, rather unusually, lights up a slim cigarette, pre-coital and not post. She wants to talk but is too distracted to listen to my answers.

"Are you ok? You seem a little distracted?" I say as I begin to take off my tie.

"Oh, I'm fine. I just heard from an old friend on my way over here. It was unexpected and not particularly welcome." She sashay's over to me, starker's, and tops up my glass with the remaining wine.

"You would have made a fabulous geisha," I say, admiring her beautiful body as she serves my drink.

"Anata no sabicu de imu", she purrs with a little bow, her tits falling forward, one nipple grazing my cab sav.

"Impressive," I say, referring to the Japanese and not the nipples, although they too are spectacularly impressive.

"I worked in Tokyo for a couple of years… back in the day", I flex, hoping to impress.

"Didn't we all" she dismisses without further explanation. "Now, come and lay down. You look like you could use a massage."

The two nights I have with her each week are the highlight of my week, and although killing me financially, she's worth every penny.

She takes out a bottle of expensive-looking oil from her bag. It's a treat she repeats often, and it sure as hell works for me. She never skimps on the oil either… no basic wholesale rubbish… it's always expensive and smells incredible. Something fancy from Space NK, according to the bag, and I wonder if she factors the price of her oil into my bill each week, I wouldn't put it past her, the cheeky bitch. I don't care. It's very girlfriend behaviour.

"Before you do that, let's take a dip in the tank," I say…jumping up enthusiastically and pressing my hard-on back down. If I didn't dip it into the water soon, the night would be over before the lid from the oil was off.

JASON

Friday

The old stairwell is completely out of bounds for guests and staff… unless in the event of a fire. Jason ignored this stupid rule at all times; it was the only way of snooping around the hotel corridors without being seen. He always made sure the appropriate security cameras were switched off first. Carefully he selected the correct screens for each floor he planned to roam, before taking himself off to the stairwell.

Occasionally he would wander down to the basement floor to take a look at the women in the gym. Or even better still, he would head across to the swimming pool, a good perch for catching sight of them in their cosies. On other nights he preferred to see who was hanging around in the bar or the fancy Hux restaurant. His favourite thing though was to wander unseen around the empty, dimly lit corridors, idly guessing who was behind each bedroom door and imagining what the hell those minted scumbags were up to inside.

CHAPTER 8

AMANDA

Friday

I pour Teddy another large glass of wine; the poor guy looks like he needs it. Gulping back a glass of sparkling water, I perch on the edge of the large bed.

Teddy isn't the only one feeling stressed tonight. Jimmy's constant messages were giving me endless sleepless nights and constant paranoia. I felt exhausted but wired.

I seemed to have fallen so far behind old friends who had settled with husbands, flourishing careers or babies. I was alone and still renting because I liked the temporary; it felt safer to me, knowing I could leave.

I had a constant itch that couldn't be scratched. A need for change. I couldn't remember feeling any sort of contentment since being a kid… before my brother Ben died.

Suicide leaves a terrible lifetime of unanswered questions. Knowing that someone you loved so fiercely felt so unhappy and desperate that dying was their best option…it was enough to kill the entire family in its wake. It was a lifelong burden of guilt that ate away at your core.

The closest I had come to real happiness had been falling in love with Ben's best friend. We offered comfort to each other in the years after his death, keeping his memory alive through our togetherness. I couldn't do that with anyone else, and still couldn't, as they didn't know Ben or understand what I had been through.

When his friend broke things off and left me for Uni, I was bereft all over again. I had never wanted another boyfriend since, and certainly not a husband; no one could compare. Someone new would never know Ben; they couldn't help me keep him alive. How could anyone offer that again?

I decided not to bother with Uni…I was too depressed and already dabbling in recreational drugs to try and numb the hole left by Ben. Instead, I took a job in promotions which was great for me as I had to be cheerful, sociable, and put on my make-up…it made me engage.

It was at one of the sports hospitality events that I had been approached by a well-dressed woman who talked to me about the 'discreet' and high-end escort service she ran. She casually suggested we meet for a coffee later that week.

Intrigued, I agreed. She was smart and sassy and talked through the surprisingly straightforward set-up. It certainly sounded appealing. Nothing untoward, just accompanying wealthy businessmen who needed somebody beautiful, bright and educated to hold a decent conversation with their clients… without emotional complications. There was no sex involved or expected… unless I wanted there to be, and should that be the case, I could charge triple my fee.

It blew my mind that this work even existed. The money was great. It paid my rent, allowed me to travel, to buy beautiful clothes, and it funded my growing penchant for party drugs and good times to escape the sadness.

Meeting Jimmy at one of the many parties had been instrumental in life taking a turn for the worse.

Jimmy was clever…everyone's best friend, full of life, kind, inclusive, hilarious and always there to help any of his 'friends' should they need a bed for the night, some cash to tide them over or a free gram of coke.

Thanks to him, innocent escort work soon scaled up from topical conversation to so much more. Addicts need money. Nobody knew how bad it got. I kept it together, always well dressed, smart, 'normal' for want of a better word. I was your nice neighbour, the pretty girl that jogged past you each morning; I wasn't who you thought.

Then something unexpected happened; the hand of fate had stepped in…the universe had listened and sent him back to me. For the second time in my life, Ben's best friend was going to make everything ok again… but this time he didn't even know it yet.

According to my cousin, he was back living in London after a decade working in New York, and it was all I needed to try and wean myself off this crap and get myself clean. I wanted him back, and there was no way he would consider me in this state.

I managed to book into the most expensive rehab clinic I could find over in West London and cleaned myself up once and for all.

I cut ties with anyone associated with my party days, including and specifically, Jimmy. His messages were, therefore, all the more terrifying now they had begun.

Jimmy, of course, wasn't the 'kind' friend he had seemed. He was a psychopath and was now desperate for money. He had bitten a city boy's ear off for unpaid coke money, only a few years before. You didn't say no to Jimmy, and the fear that he was watching me, following, waiting… seeped right down into my guts.

I rummage in my handbag, noticing a glint from the blade halfway down. Stuffing my scarf over the top of my kitchen knife, I push it further down into the bottom of my bag. Ridiculous really. Old and blunt from my kitchen drawer, but it offered some small comfort while Jimmy was around. I grab the beautiful neroli and lemon body oil that I have brought for Teddy and fix my face.

"Ted. Put your wine down and lay back. Time for your massage." I smile brightly, checking the clock out of the corner of my eye. I make a mental note to add another seventy quid onto his bill for the oil.

He suggests we swim naked in the tank, assuming, as always, that it's why I suggested this suite. I couldn't care less about the tank. I'm in the Duke of Shoreditch Suite for one reason and one reason only. Finally, he was back in my life, and I had tracked him down to this hotel.

Dominic Box.

JASON

Friday

Jason loitered outside The Duke of Shoreditch suite on the third floor, where Ted Villandry was shacked up with his whore.

It was the best room in the hotel by a mile, with floor-length windows on all three sides, a ginormous bed against the wall and a large glass bathtub in the middle of the room, practically a swimming pool; it was so wide. Occasionally Jason would meander past the room whilst the cleaners were in there.

Once or twice he had even managed to sweet talk his way inside the suite, offering a cigarette to one of the scrubbers that cleaned the gaff.

Ted Villandry could easily get a proper girlfriend, but Jason had never had any luck with real-life women, and working night shifts at The Huxley didn't help. Why should Teddy be able to afford hookers when he could easily get himself a normal bird, the greedy bastard.

Jason hammered his fist on their suite door in irritation and then legged it back to the stairwell, hiding and waiting for the dumb fuck to answer the door. Sure enough, a few seconds later, Teddy's messy, blonde head stuck out from behind the door, bare shoulders giving away his game and wearing a dopey look on his face as he looked left and right for the phantom knocker. Jason sniggered to himself. Who knew that knock-down ginger could be just as much fun as an adult? Fuck it. He would keep knocking until his break time was up.

CHAPTER 9

KATE

Saturday

The weekend arrives, and I'm a little restless and on edge as I potter around the kitchen, looking for idle jobs that don't need doing. My mind is filled with thoughts of Dominic. The thrill of last Thursday night together at The Huxley still burnt into my skin, and already, I'm craving the escape again.

My skin itches just under the surface. I want to eat, drink, smoke or fuck … maybe even all of the above. I can't make up my mind. I need something physical to drag me away from my scratchy thoughts.

I busy myself with cleaning the whole house from top to bottom, scrubbing at every surface with Viakal, despite our cleaner blitzing the whole house only yesterday. When I finish, I set about pulling clothes from each of our wardrobes, re-organizing them into casual and smart sections, and bagging up handfuls of stuff for charity.

I don't touch Connie's wardrobe. Her room remains exactly as it did the day she died. The prettiest room in the house with its cream and pink floral eiderdown and matching curtains. Her favourite book, the wishing chair, sits on the chest of drawers by her bed. The corner turned down on the last page that we read together. The room still smells of her, of strawberry shampoo and baby lotion and… cinnamon porridge. Sometimes panic sets in, and my chest tightens when I can't immediately smell her. I clutch at her pillow or one of her soft toys, just to grasp at her scent until my heart rate slows when I finally inhale her.

Tom says we shouldn't keep her things forever; we can't keep some weird shrine; it's unhealthy and sad for Freddie to see. He thinks other little girls would benefit from her lovely things. 'Little girls in need', he calls them. He doesn't seem to realize that I need *my* little girl. This is all I have of her, but I don't argue; I swallow down any angry or mean words and keep my silence.

I search around for more jobs, but all is well with the house; it's only my mind that's in such a mess. Bored and impatient, I open the fridge and defiantly stick my finger into a piece of leftover chocolate cake. I don't bother with a fork; instead, I scoop up a messy piece with my bare hand, cramming it into my mouth.

"What on earth are you doing?" Tom's voice startles me, and I slam the fridge door like a secret eater.

"You have chocolate all around your mouth," he says, circling his mouth with his finger to illustrate. He looks baffled and a little disgusted.

"Can I get you a plate for that?" he asks, with more concern than the deed warrants.

"Do you fancy seeing a movie tonight? I deftly change the subject, like a mad woman. I should make a little effort this weekend and try to reconnect with him in some way.

"Maybe we could grab a bite to eat?' I persist.

"I could ask Anya to babysit?"

His head is deep in the fridge, surveying the mutilation of the fudge cake. Death by chocolate.

"You've made a right old mess in here", he admonishes.

I sigh loudly like a teenage brat. Who cares about the fucking cake? My eyes roll automatically as I let out another exaggerated huff.

He wanders off, mumbling under his breath, and I stay still, gazing out to the garden and drumming my fingers impatiently on the kitchen worktop. I will not rise to his petty complaining. I want us to have a nice weekend.

I follow him like an obedient dog, down the hall and along to his study, where I repeat my suggestion to the back of his bent neck. Try again, Kate. Make an effort Kate. He's hunched over his laptop, reading glasses pushed high on the bridge of his nose and as still as a mannequin.

He doesn't answer at first, and I presume he hasn't heard, so I try a third time,

"Do you fancy"?

"Err… a movie", he finishes my sentence. "No, not tonight, Kate; I've got loads to do. I need to finish this presentation for tomorrow. I told you it's a really big case, this one. Why don't you see if Jules wants to go with you?

He doesn't turn around, and I stay still in the doorway for a few minutes before I go into the kitchen and snatch my phone from the charger.

I hit WhatsApp and type furiously,

'Hey, I know it's the weekend, but is there any chance you could sneak out tonight? Love to see you. K xx'

I hate that I am feeling and sounding needier with Dominic as the months go by. This wasn't how it was supposed to be; I don't want to start caring for him; I can't. I just can't.

I see him typing back instantly, and I can't help the warmth that fills me as I watch the flashing bubble appear.

D. Moby

'Hey! Unexpected …but yes!! Can't get away for an overnighter… movie and a bite to eat?"

I smile widely.

Please tell me how this can be wrong.

We meet in Notting Hill and head up to the Electric cinema. The old cinema is dangerously small, yet somehow safer than the large, overcrowded Odeon in town. The fear of us seeing someone is only outweighed by the fear of them seeing us without our knowledge.

The film is quite good, a psychological thriller with Vincent Cassel. It's in French with subtitles, and so it takes a little more concentration than normal, which is nigh on impossible when his hands are all over me.

I hold my breath for what feels like hours as his hand runs up the inside of my thigh, under my long, loose skirt, gently pulling the edge of my knickers across to one side. Subconsciously I must have worn a skirt for this very reason. It's the middle of winter, and my legs are bare and wide. I breathe heavily like a randy adolescent on the back row as he fingers me gently, all the while never taking his own eyes off the movie.

We skip dinner due to gorging on too many disgusting nachos and instead grab a quick glass of wine at the bar next door. Sinking into cosy armchairs, we stare at each other over the top of our wine glasses. I try to hold on to this feeling, this intoxication and obsession. I know this feeling won't last, it never does, but for now, it's the only thing I can really feel.

"Where did you tell her you were going tonight?" I ask with a sudden twinge of curiosity. I never, ever mention his wife or life outside this bubble, and he looks puzzled by my unusual interest.

"I said I was out with James, one of the dads from school. You?"

"Seeing a movie at the electric …with Jules."

He nods, and I sip my wine, taking a furtive glance around the bar. It's full of media types gesticulating wildly as they listen only to the sound of their own voices. I envy their uncomplicated lives. The only thing they have to worry about is which fancy members club to carry on to or whether to order the Hendricks or the Monkey forty-seven. Big decisions. When did life become so hard? Why was life so much harder for some than others?

I stifle a yawn, suddenly tired from all the chaos within me, the over-active adrenalin buzz from earlier finally fizzes out like a used sparkler, and I feel depleted.

"Let's get you home, sleeping beauty" He drains the last of his wine and orders us an Uber to share.

We French kiss for the entire journey home until the Uber comes to a stop, and we pull over into the street just before mine. He asks the driver to give us a minute before grabbing the side of my face again with his right hand, turning me towards him and gently licking around the inside of my mouth with his tongue. The electricity sizzles, and I let myself out of the car quickly before I'm carried away once more.

"See you at the Huxley…Thursday," he calls through the half-open window as the Uber heads off to his house in the opposite direction.

When I let myself in, I'm surprised to see Tom sprawled on the sofa, also watching a movie and dipping into a selection of snacks which are artfully laid out in front of him…leftovers from the last 'Pink Pig' event. He doesn't look busy to me, and he sure as hell isn't working on any presentation.

I want to be angry, to be disappointed, to shout and accuse, but I have no right, no right whatsoever. I wander into the kitchen and spot his unfinished presentation lying on top of the counter.

I open the fridge and take out the leftover chocolate cake; grabbing a small handful and squeezing it tightly into my palm, I watch blankly as the sticky fudge squelches underneath my nails, turning them black. I turn and lift up the top few sheaves of paper before I smear my chocolate-filled hand down the centre of the fourth or fifth page of his document. I wash my hands and head straight up to bed as more deafening silence fills our strange home.

CHAPTER 10

DOMINIC

Saturday

"That was James on the phone. He's asked if I fancy joining him and a couple of the other guys for a quiz… down at The Ship Inn. Do you mind? You look quite knackered, to be honest…are you ok."

Helena is lying under the faux fur throw, staring blankly at some Netflix box set she has locked herself into.

"Do as you like," she says without looking up.

"You've got to stop this, Helena…I try so hard with you; nothing pleases you. Why don't you go and take the kids up to your mum's for the holidays? Get some rest?"

I don't hear the rest of her words; I'm halfway up the stairs.

I quickly shower and change before going online to book us two executive seats, sitting at the back of the electric on Portobello.

I arrive at the cinema, and Kate looks sexy as fuck in a long, flowing skirt and a huge chunky sweater, arriving seconds before the movie is due to start.

We head to the kiosk to grab some of their ropey snacks. She draws the line at the colourless, meatless hot dogs, but meets me half-way with nachos. I grab us a bottle of wine and two glasses, and we head to the back row like a pair of naughty teens.

"Just one glass for you...you said yourself that your tummy was getting a little bloated from our weekly champagne", I remind her, patting it lightly through her jumper. Any excuse to get my hands on her.

I have no idea what the film was about, something French and pretentious, but I didn't take any of it in as I was too busy reciting church hymns to prevent my cock from bursting out of my jeans and exploding into the nachos. The touch of her drove me wild, and knowing we wouldn't even get to have sex tonight made it even more intense.

Afterwards, we grab a couple of drinks in the fancy bar next door, which is rammed with idiots. Jumped-up creatives, full of shit, heads so far up their own photo-shopped arses. I can barely hear a word she says, as they are so loud and rah.

So, when Kate asks what my alibi for the evening is, I have to double-check that's what she asked. It's unlike her to give a toss about what I tell Helena; it's usually me asking questions. I don't like her asking; I've got one nosey wife, and I don't need to answer to another, but she catches me off guard, so I tell her the truth.

I take the hint when she starts yawning, and I'm pretty knackered myself after several sleepless nights thinking about this mess. I've spent all week wondering whether I could even afford a divorce… if there is actually a way of properly swapping Helena for Kate on a permanent basis for an easier life and, frankly, better sex.

The trouble was I would end up having to give most of what I have to Helena; isn't that how it works? I'm starting to think my own Dad wasn't so cowardly after all; maybe he didn't take the easy option leaving my mother without a backward glance. It would have been much easier to stay in every conceivable way. I drain my drink and order us an Uber.

When I get home, the lights are out, and Helena is already in bed, asleep. I stick my head around the door of each of the kid's bedrooms and feel a slight pang of guilt. I brush it off and head up to the spare room on the top floor. I never sleep in the spare room, it's a bit of a statement, and Helena will think it strange. I'll no doubt pay for it tomorrow with more questions and accusations from her, but for the first time, it doesn't feel right to climb into bed next to her. I'm starting to think it's time Kate chose me over Tom.

The next morning the house is empty. Helena has taken the girls out shopping and dropped Max off at his football training. I pour myself a nice, real coffee and settle at the breakfast bar for a read of the sports section. That's when I see it. The bright, neon pink post it. Shaped like a flamingo and ripped out of Amalie's new birthday notepad. It is stuck to the fridge door with my name in capitals, followed by a short message underneath.

'James called last night… while you were out with him. H '

CHAPTER 11

TEDDY

Saturday

It's my weekend with the kids, which always perks me up... although they aren't really kids anymore. They prefer to live in their own home with Suzie...instead of meeting me for pizza, a movie or brunch in town on my designated weekend. There are no sleepovers, and none of their clothes or belongings littering my floor as a warm reminder of their presence... in my life or home. It hurts, but it's just as well, bearing in mind the rabbit hutch I now call home.

I pull up outside my beautiful, old home that sits just off Chiswick High Road. It's a sprawling, Edwardian house, impressive to look at and with five huge bedrooms that span out over the second and third floors. The floor-to-ceiling windows breathe the most incredible light into the front sitting room and all the way out to the breakfast room, but the house is afforded just enough privacy by the pretty oak tree that sits proudly up front, decorated with twinkling fairy lights, shading the movements inside.

Funny how I never once stopped to notice how incredible this house was when I actually lived in it. I had been far too busy to notice anything outside of my office. Now, every time I pull up outside, the thought smashes me right in the face.

I was no longer the perfect guy with the perfect wife and children; I was just the douche funding it all.

I'm suddenly reminded of my counsellor and her 'mindfulness' chats.

"Live in the moment and be grateful, Teddy…Oh, and don't forget to buy more joss sticks on your way out."

I yank a fat, yellow, rose head from Suzie's prize bush in irritation as I march up the drive, cursing as I prick my damn thumb. I stuff the broken flower into my pocket.

"Hey Lucy, how are you darling? Is Mum home?"

I squeeze my daughter as she flings open the door, looking disappointed that it's only me and not the Hermes delivery guy she expected. She isn't so little anymore at almost eighteen, but she's still *my* little girl all the same. God, I missed being around the kids every day. Even though half of the time we had all been so busy with our lives that we had merely brushed past each other in the hallway in a daily rush, it had still been nice knowing they were here, somewhere in the house, breathing in the same air as me. I hate living alone. Hate it. I head past her at the front door and back into my old home.

"She's in the kitchen making breakfast," Lucy mumbles, heading back up to her room and back to bed, presumably. It's still only eleven am, so practically the middle of the night for most teens on a Saturday.

"Teddy", Suzie beams with genuine fondness as I come into the sunny, extended kitchen, the one that I lovingly paid for right before she asked me to leave. She gives me a friendly hug and pours me a fresh coffee. It smells divine. It smells like home.

"How are things?" she asks, pulling up her barstool to the impressive island that my salary built.

Suzie looked great for forty-five. She had a few fine lines here and there but was still just as beautiful to me, with her vivid red, long, thick hair and porcelain skin. She's often likened to Julianne Moore, which she modestly denies but secretly loves.

"Yeah, not bad, not bad," I say…looking around the place for evidence of the arsehole in residence. "Is Giles not over today, then?" I ask innocently.

Suzie likes to refer to Giles as her 'partner'. She once told me that 'boyfriend' sounded silly at her age. I had given her a scathing look and told her in no uncertain terms, "If you ask me, 'partner' sounds like you're now a raving dyke". She had eyed me coolly and replied,

"But nobody did ask you, Teddy'.

"Err…yes, he's upstairs, just getting changed". She says. "He'll be down in a minute. We're going over to Lorna and Mick's for lunch."

I pull out the virtual knife she's just plunged into my spinal cord and picture our oldest friends, Lorna and Mick, laughing and entertaining that prick in their beautiful home. I take a larger-than-intended swig of coffee in sheer irritation, immediately spitting it out as it burns the hell out of my tongue. "SHIIIIIIIIITTTTTTTT" I shout, grabbing a glass and filling it with water as I plunge my blistered tongue into it.

"Are you ok, Teddy?" The arseholes cut glass voice pierces both the room and the main artery in my neck in one clean octave.

"Fine, thanks, mate." I stick an emphasis on mate as I eyeball him and wipe my mouth on the back of my hand, a defiant and admittedly childish act of fuck you.

"I had lunch with Lucinda Jones last week", Suzie blusters on, oblivious to any animosity.

"And?" I say flatly, my politeness in remission due to the Giles-shaped, cancerous growth that has entered my lymph nodes.

Lucinda Jones is the spoilt, but admittedly, fun wife of one of my oldest, wealthiest clients at D&K. Seb Jones and I are not best friends, but we do get on pretty well and have been to various dinners together over the years, where the wives seemed to hit it off straight away.

'Is everything ok with you, Teddy? You aren't in any trouble at work, are you? Lucinda was a little quiet. She mentioned that Seb was concerned about some money trouble. Not sure if she meant *your* money or *his*? Have you spoken to him recently?' Suzie pulls a stool up next to me.

"Really?" I say, a little bored. "The only trouble Seb has is worrying about what to spend his money on next. Probably having a mid-life crisis or shagging his secretary," I add bitchily.

Giles lets out an unexpected guffaw at this, and both Suzie and I shoot him a look of contempt for our own different reasons.

"Anyway, is George ready…we need to get going," I say impatiently. ' The Chelsea match is at three, and I would like us to grab lunch together beforehand." I help myself to another fresh coffee whilst using my side eye to read a random invitation, lying on the worktop, addressed to 'Suzie and Giles'. The vein in my forehead pulsates.

"I'll go and grab George for you," Giles says cordially.

"No, you won't. I'll get my own son, thank you." I flounce off with my hot mouth and even hotter head, unintentionally wafting three large yellow petals from my coat pocket and onto the parquet floor as I slam the door.

Arsehole.

CHAPTER 12

AMANDA

Saturday

It's Saturday lunchtime, and I'm sitting at the back of The Iris café in Holborn.

The Iris is Dominic's local and just around the corner from his office. I followed him here this morning, straight from his home in Clapham and then first to his fancy health club. Having waited for an hour and a half outside his gym, I then drove slowly behind him as he made his way to the office.

I settled myself in The Iris café, knowing at some point he would come in for a coffee or a bite as was his routine, and sure enough, here he was.

I'm hidden away at a tiny formica table in the far left corner when I spot him striding in, taking up all the air and space as he always did. He orders a panini and hands over his card. Even from here, I can tell that he's flirting with the waitress, and I feel amused and irritated in equal measure. I cover most of my face with my phone, hunching over what's left of my lukewarm cappuccino. With no-one on the other end of the line, I'm feeling faintly ridiculous at the lengths I've gone to.

It had taken months of hanging around outside his office before I eventually spotted him one lunchtime, heading over to The Iris.

He still looked magnificent. There was no other word for it.

The café was a small artisan hive of activity due to the wonderful charisma of Federico, the Italian owner and his two beautiful daughters. The daughters held court, chatting and flirting with man, woman or beast whilst serving delicious, traditional food.

I quickly discovered he lived in Clapham, in a very large and very beautiful house, just off the common. He went to a very expensive health club at least six mornings a week and always grabbed a coffee from the small stand in Battersea Rise, just by the florist.

Rather surprisingly, he seemed to be visiting some kind of counsellor or therapist in Marylebone, always on a Wednesday at nine. This suggested all was not as well as it appeared in that big, beautiful home. More surprising were his regular trips to a little-known hotel in East London called The Huxley. Every Thursday, he would head there after work. I hadn't yet followed him inside the Hotel, but had watched his grey overcoat disappearing up the stone steps and into the foyer on many an occasion. I could only presume it was one of those tedious 'date nights' that married couples liked to harp on about.

'Keeping the wheels on', the older women at my gym called it, as they talked loudly over their post-pilates lattes.

I suggested to Teddy that we try this 'Huxley Hotel' instead of our usual place in Covent Garden, and of course, Teddy was as compliant and polite as ever. So far, I've refrained from staying on the same night as Dominic, as I'm enjoying staying in his favourite suite, feeling close to him before I feel confident enough to face him. I can't bear to see him there with his wife, and I sure as hell don't want him to see me with Teddy.

I gaze at the back of his neck as he pays. He stands out a country mile against other bland, lesser men.

His tall body is clad in a fitted, grey cashmere sweater and blue jeans. He is dark and moody, exactly how I remember him and my stomach flutters as does somewhere a little lower.

I've had my hair newly cut at an expensive salon and gone back to the heavy French fringe he always preferred. He would laugh endlessly when we were younger at my 'spam' forehead and tell me to cut it… so I'm feeling good and as close as possible to how he would remember me.

My phone unexpectedly pings in my earlobe, and I jump slightly before sneaking a quick glance at the new message. Jimmy!!

God, the man was relentless. Day and night, his messages were taunting me, a reminder of the impossible amount of money he had decided I owed him.

I dart behind the lunch menu as I see Dominic turn this way. At one point, he appears to look directly at me but doesn't notice me, my hair hidden under my beanie hat, covering all traces of blonde. He winks at the pretty Italian waitress and strides out to the pavement, oblivious of my presence.

I leave right behind him, keeping out of sight but watching, waiting and drinking in every inch of him. I'm amazed he hasn't spotted me. He heads back to the office, so I decide to head off to my own, less swanky gym and burn off some steam.

My thoughts are dominated by him, and I'm wondering why on earth he would waste his Saturday in the office…avoiding home, maybe? Wishful thinking.

I stand in front of the washbasin and adjust my long, blonde ponytail. The woman next to me, stares at me through the mirror, but I take no notice. I'm used to being looked at by men and women. She flicks her tap on full but stupidly presses her hand too close to the faucet, spraying the water upwards and over my gym vest and face.

"What the hell…." I wipe my eye with the back of my hand. "Watch it," I add, annoyed. I have light make up on despite being about to work out, and I can already see a smudge of wet mascara forming under my eye. I tut with irritation.

"Sorry. It was an accident," she says, eyeballing me. She looks anything but sorry as she marches off towards the gym, looking mildly pleased with herself.

She looked vaguely familiar… probably one of those café gossips, droning on about their marriages.

CHAPTER 13

KATE

Sunday

Connie's birthday arrives on Sunday and hits me like a freight train as I open my heavy lids with a familiar dread. I wake to an unseasonably warm morning for mid-November. The sky is clear and the palest of blue, dotted with occasional yet perfect marshmallow clouds, and I feel her all around me, bringing the sunshine with her, just as she had done in life. The air is warm, almost humid, the way it feels and smells when you step off a plane in Southern Spain or Italy, sweet, burnt and dense.

The crisp, golden leaves that have scattered and gathered under the trees are at odds with this otherwise summer's day.

I lay very still in our bed, unable to move. Connie would have been twelve today and on the cusp of blossoming into a young woman. She would only be a couple of months into her new secondary school and already so much more grown up just for being there.

No doubt she would be starting to challenge the status quo, as is the way at that tricky age. Her and I would no doubt have clashed over clothes and rules and mess, arguing over all of those silly stresses and worries that actually mean nothing in the end. Who cared if she left her bed unmade as long as she was alive? What did it matter if she came home thirty minutes after her curfew as long as she still breathed the same air as us? Why worry if her future boyfriend was a little rough around the edges, if he made her smile? As long as it meant she was here with me, living and breathing, it wouldn't have mattered.

Every fibre in my body ached with anger and frustration, sadness and pity over what might have been, what should have been and all the things she and I would miss together because of being in the wrong place at the wrong time. It wasn't fair, it would never make sense, and I would never be at peace with it. I would always wonder why her? I would always feel this utter emptiness and a million other emotions besides, which I couldn't even begin to understand or articulate. I would die for the chance to have her fight with me. I try hard to picture her at twelve years old but try as I might, she is forever eight in my head and heart. She cartwheels in front of me, blonde hair swinging upside down, laughing loudly and carelessly as she spins over and over on the lawn.

I don't cry. I have no tears left. Instead, I harden the wall around my heart, and my eyes stay dry as old bones as I gear myself up to face the day. It's the only way to keep on walking through the fire. If I care, I'll crumble. There will be calls and messages and cards today… checking we are ok, everyone thinking of us and offering to pop over with flowers or cake or cuddles. Although so very kind, I dread all of them. I don't want kindness. I want Connie.

Tom walks into the room with a towel wrapped around his waist, his hair wet from the shower.

"Hey, fancy a coffee?" he asks, smiling brightly.

I want to kill him.

"You do know what day it is?" My voice is as cold as steel, and my green eyes feel black and hard.

He sits on the edge of the bed and sighs heavily.

"Of course, I know what day it is, Kate." He sounds angry and accusatory… How dare he?

"So, why aren't you even acknowledging her, Tom? Why are you asking me about coffee in that cheery fucking voice?" I demand irrationally, with a lump in my throat that is so hard it physically hurts to swallow it down.

"Forget it," he says, looking at me with bewilderment and slamming our bedroom door on his way out.

I remain still for hours. I stare up at the ceiling while Tom carries on with the day and its demands. He takes Freddie over to his little friend's birthday party, pops to the supermarket, busies himself with errands and even plays music in the kitchen. All around, life goes on, and I don't know how or why this is even possible for anyone, least of all Tom.

My phone beeps around one o'clock, and it's Dominic.

WhatsApp

D Moby

"*Kate. I know it's a difficult day, but I'm free for drinks or a nice slow fuck later if you want to escape. D* "

I nearly throw up at the insensitivity of him…what is wrong with him? I shake it off, I'm being oversensitive; he was obviously trying to cheer me up and lighten the mood… bad timing, not his fault. I clutch at my stomach, feeling a slight roll there… he's right; I am drinking too much.

I lay numb for another hour, thinking of Connie, of Freddie, of the four of us… of the three of us…

my body aches on and on until I finally agree to a walk and a coffee with Jules after some persuasion from Tom. She's the only friend who knows about Dominic, the only person I don't have to lie to.

We meet outside the cafe by the Bayswater tube and cross over into Hyde Park, her arm linked through mine.

"So, come on, missy… how is he?" She hands me a takeaway latte.

"Tom? Oh, cheery as ever…barely registered the day Jules. If it wasn't for Freddie…I swear I would have to go."

"Nooooo... not Tom... Mr Big... Mr Box... Mr Big-Box!," she roars with laughter at her own little joke and pokes me in the ribs. I can't help but laugh with her.

"Ohhh right… yeah… Mr Box is good; he's lovely actually… he even remembered it's her anniversary and sent a nice message." I say

She stops still in the park and let's go of my arm,

"OH, MY GOD. You're falling for him, aren't you?? Shit, Kate, this is serious… this isn't just sex.

Do you love him?"

"Nooooo, I don't know, I don't… I can't; I can't even go there. Our family's been destroyed already, and I can't have what's left of it destroyed again. It isn't fair."

"But what about you, darling?" She links my arm again and strokes it softly with her other hand. "What about what's fair for you? You deserve to be happy, you know. You *are* allowed."

"I don't want to talk about it, Jules. It makes me feel physically ill… it's too much. Please…tell me something fun…how was your Hinge date last night?

"Weeell…he looked at least 30 years older than his profile picture; he had been married three times. What else? Oh yeah…he insisted we order Veurve Cliquot all night, then discovered he'd forgotten his wallet, so guess who picked up the £300 tab?"

"Nooooo…oh God, what an asshole…what was his name??"

"Dick," She says…screwing her face up. "Richard…but his friends call him Dick…can you believe that. Who the hell calls themself Dick?"

"Turpin??" I suggest.

"Exactly…thieving bastard!!" She shouts …before we bend double with laughter. I don't know when the laughter turns into crying, but without knowing, I am on my knees in the park with Jules wrapped around me as we both cry and cry for what feels like hours.

CHAPTER 14

DOMINIC

Sunday

Helena is upstairs packing for her and the kids. They will head to her Mothers in the morning for the week.

I'm twitchy, stressed, bored…and horny.

I consider a quick look on Pornhub or Hinge but decide to drop Kate a message instead to see if she's up for a little afternoon delight.

I'm just typing out something about a blow job when I remember it's her kid's birthday or anniversary, maybe …fuck, I can't remember which.

I delete the message quickly and re-type, telling her I know how difficult the day must be. I suggest we hook up anyway for a cheeky shag as I know it will cheer her up, and plus …I'm hoping she can meet these next few days while I have a pink pass.

It had near broken Kate and Tom and had broken the driver, who was well into his eighties. It was nobody's fault, and yet there was a need to blame. The old man blamed himself and had died within the year, most probably from the stress. For Kate, it was crucial that somebody took responsibility for what happened. Tom had looked away for just a few seconds, and from what I could gather from Kate's defensive responses…Tom didn't seem *sad enough* anymore; he had forgiven himself too easily and too quickly.

I made the mistake of fighting his corner, playing devil's advocate. I thought it might help her move on if she could understand his grief too …plus this was when I didn't want her getting any ideas about leaving him for me. I suggested that maybe his practical solutions were *his* way of coping, but she wouldn't have it. She was angry and upset and made it very clear that the topic was off-limits. Fine by me, to be honest.

"Shall we go for a bite to eat tonight before I leave with the kids in the morning?"

The sound of Helena's hopeful voice interrupts my daydream, and I realize that I'm staring into space, out through our kitchen window. My glass over-flows with water from the continuous, running tap. Her voice is soft and gentle, and I feel the unexpected touch of her hand on my arm, for the first time in months. I'm so shocked; I pull back as if she has scolded me with boiling water. It's a natural instinct, but the hurt on her face slaps my own with shame. She has no right to make me feel bad or mean… how dare she? I'm furious.

"Oh, what now??? What have I done wrong now? You always try and start a fight over nothing," I tell her, irritated. For fuck's sake, I hadn't intentionally pulled my hand from her.

She's already walking away, and I slam my glass down in fury.

"Forget it. I'm tired anyway," she mumbles, grabbing her gym bag and car keys and slamming the door shut behind her.

She hadn't said a word about the other night or the note on the fridge, so I hadn't mentioned it either. I was being paranoid, and no wonder.

"SHHHHIIIIIIT" I shout into the empty room. I rub my face with both hands. This can't go on; I have to do something about this mess; she's getting more and more difficult by the day. Today is not the right day, though.

I put my phone down on the kitchen table and notice Tom Golding's business card sticking out from my wallet.

I hadn't intended to meet Tom. I guess curiosity about her husband had got the better of me, and so I had made an excuse to go and see his law firm a few months ago. I had made an appointment with a colleague of his, a fellow lawyer, whom I told I wanted to discuss the financial implications for a possible divorce. Really, I had hoped to catch a glimpse of the opposition, see him in action in his own habitat. It was a male ego thing, competitive…but I hadn't planned on actually speaking with the prick. I was caught off guard when the receptionist told me that my lawyer had been held up in court with another client, and so Tom Golding would be seeing me today.

No sooner had I digested the news and stood up, ready to leave, than there he was, striding towards me, arm outstretched, introducing himself with a broad smile as he pumped my hand.

I made the meeting as short and sweet as possible, so much so that I could see he was visibly annoyed and thought me a time waster. I felt irritated by *his* irritation, and my natural reaction was to say something cocky and cutting… but then I remembered I was screwing his wife, and for once, I held my tongue.

The brief meeting had got me thinking though…I think I would get her to leave the smarmy bastard. I needed to look into the implications of divorcing Helena and what that would mean for me financially. I decide to message my old friend, Will from Uni, the only other lawyer I know. I could do with a little 'off the record' chat with him about things at home, and I send him a quick message to suggest that we meet for lunch, explaining I could use some practical and legal advice. I mention lightly that I'm having issues with Helena, but I don't mention Kate or anything of an affair. Will responds straight away with a wide-eyed emoji. You wouldn't imagine he's a highly credited lawyer by his text banter, but I smile at his juvenile and familiar response. We arrange to meet the following Thursday for lunch at my local, The Iris café, right next to my office. Things need to move forward.

CHAPTER 15

TEDDY

Saturday

I drop George home to Suzie after the Chelsea game and head back to my miserable flat for the afternoon. I'm restless and have an uneasy feeling nestling in my gut after speaking to Suzie. I need to call Seb again. It would be harder for him to avoid me at home on the weekend.

"Seeeeb", I sing song with exaggerated bonhomie as he finally takes my call.

"Ted", he replies flatly.

At last, I've got hold of the son of a bitch.

My palms sweat as I grip the phone a little tighter. Initially, I hadn't thought much of it when Suzie mentioned her lunch with Lucinda and flagged up some kind of problem with Seb.

Then it dawned on me that he hadn't returned any of my calls for a few weeks now. The son of a bitch was ghosting me.

No reply to any calls or e-mails over the last week or two, and the realization filled my bowels with a sudden and uneasy dread.

Once the paranoia set in, it was all I could think about, and I pretty much missed the match as I scrawled through my phone to see when Seb had last responded. George was pissed off with my distraction and told me off for always being on my phone; our roles reversed yet again. It was becoming harder and harder not to feel like a failure and downright imbecile around the kids these days, but I needed to know if Seb knew what I'd been up to at work.

"I thought we might have lunch this week and catch up on your investment and current share prices?" I suggest, with more joviality than a game show host.

"No need Ted. I'm meeting Charles this week to talk numbers." Seb delivers his killer blow like a toneless Darlek, and the word 'Exterminate' pops into my head and makes me laugh nervously.

A cluster of nerve-endings begin to gather and multiply, forming a hard lump in the pit of my thyroid. Seb is my oldest and wealthiest client. He's sort of a friend, for Christ's sake. We've had countless dinners over the years, not to mention family get-togethers, golf days and even that long weekend in Edinburgh with the wives and kids. He has certainly never, ever felt the need to go above my head and speak to Charles in all these years. I falter for a few seconds before recovering my game-show banter.

"Oh, excellent. In fact, I only said to Charles last week that it would be great for you guys to finally meet. I'm glad he called you."

"*I* called *him*." He deadpans.

I try not to overthink his scary tone and blunder on whilst corpsing live on stage.

"How's Lucinda? The kids?" I falter, attempting to get back onto the proverbial bed with him and bounce him like a baby on our shared memory foam. Burp up a little loyalty, perhaps.

"Look, Teddy, I'm rather busy, so I'm going to have to go" He cuts me short, and I try not to gasp from the fresh wound.

"Sure. Yes, of course… well, look, let's catch up after your meeting with…" The line is dead… so am I, it would appear.

Panic rises through my shirt and pours streaming tears down my back, soaking my shirt. Seb knows what I've been up to. He must do.

Salty sweat gushes from my armpits until my white shirt is covered in transparent, messy patches.

I pace up and down my shoebox lounge before grabbing the half bottle of vodka from the kitchen cupboard. I take a neat, generous swig and try and work my way back through the clues like Scooby fucking doo.

Seb must have realized that something was amiss with his account. "You do the maths Charles… Ted is on the take", I imagined him telling my boss as he inhaled gravely on his stinking cigar whilst snaking me out.

"The disloyal cunt", I shout to the empty lounge… with all the hypocrisy of a liar caught in his own headlights.

CHAPTER 16

AMANDA

Saturday

I reapply my smudged mascara and head back from the ladies through to the busy changing room.

If I stood any chance of being with Dominic again, I needed not just a firm ass but also a proper job, and that spurred me on with my course. As soon as I qualified as a reflexologist, I planned to stop this escorting nonsense once and for all and live like a normal woman. I just had to keep going long enough to pay Jimmy off.

Once I had a respectable job, a real boyfriend and no drugs, I could go home to my family with my head held high. They loved me regardless, but I avoided visiting them anymore as I felt so deeply ashamed. They had been through enough heartache with Ben; they didn't deserve to have a daughter like me.

The changing room as always, was full of the yummy mummy brigade…the gym was their full-time job, and social scene rolled into one, and they all seemed to know one another…it was yet another clique I couldn't crack. Sometimes it felt hard to fit into any group in this life. Loneliness felt shameful… nobody would expect an attractive young woman to be so lonely; I covered it well, at least.

I notice the woman who splashed me at the sink earlier. She dresses slowly whilst glaring at me from her corner by the lockers. What was her problem? She was actually still attractive for her age, although far too skinny, it hardened her lovely face. I beam at her kindly, but she eyeballs me back. Maybe she could see right through me, see what kind of terrible job I did, what terrible life I led; maybe she could smell the lonely oddness from all the way over there. I feel judged and defensive as I march past her and head into Tums and Bums.

CHAPTER 17

KATE

Wednesday

Almost at the first session, Dr Steinberg had taken me much further back than Connie's death. She held my virtual hand and gently led me back through my own childhood. If she was disappointed to hear I didn't have any classic "Mother issues", then she didn't say.

"We get on great," I told her truthfully. However, I noticed a flurry of writing at the mention of my parent's divorce.

Dr Steinberg's pencil went into overdrive at this nugget, and I watched listlessly as it jolted back and forward, making whipping sounds against the paper.

She was no doubt concluding some kind of daddy issue, a need for safety from a man or maybe two in my case.

The world below danced to the beat of a different drum as the hustle and bustle of giddy workers clashed perversely against our quiet room. Pouring out of Hyde Park and spilling onto the pavement, they chatted with excitement whilst finishing off their packaged sandwiches in the unusual November sun.

I sat still, safe behind the large sash windows. This beautiful Grade II listed building that housed so many of my secrets.

As she scribbled, her eyes never left mine, and instead, they gently nodded and encouraged me to "go on..."

She pushed of course…wanting to know the ins and outs? Who left who and why? I danced around the question like a gifted politician. She was trying to find any other reason, aside from Connie, for my careless behaviour… but there wasn't one. I let my mind drift back out onto the street below.

As the weeks went by, Dr Steinberg moved on to Tom and how he and I had first met at work. Almost fifteen years ago, we had both started out as graduate trainees at the prestigious "Beaumont & Garrison" law firm in the city. We were clever, hungry and driven. Cocky and naïve in equal measures and the excitement of a new adult world dangled like a poisonous apple.

The arrogance of youth…I miss it. Anything felt possible, and we were invincible. Our colloquial hometowns were quickly forgotten as we pretentiously swapped bottled beer and student bars for dry white wine and smoky City bars. It was new and exciting, but it flew by far too quickly.

She asked about our sex life (what is it with shrinks). I told her honestly there had been no problem in that department, thank you very much, not until after the accident with Connie.

There is nothing sexy about grief. Fact. The statistics are not good for couples staying together after losing a child. Our hearts and minds were broken… still are.

For me, it felt disloyal to Connie even to smile at something beautiful or silly, let alone show each other real joy or physical pleasure. Impossible when she had been ripped from our lives. That was reserved for somebody who had nothing to do with Connie, a different world. Never the twain.

In the home and inside the marriage, grief lay heavy in my bones.

Tom was a different beast. Sometimes he teetered on the verge of being very happy, even in those early months. He never mentioned Connie…ever. He never asked how I felt or reminisced over any happy memories of her. His happiness made me hate him at times. Why didn't he howl like a wounded animal in the night? How could he still take pleasure in his work? How could he smile and suggest holidays and going to restaurants when all I wanted was to lie down and die? He should have felt the same; if anything, he should have felt worse. His stoic strength was his second biggest betrayal to Connie.

Tom could offer neither comfort nor escape. He was too close and too intricately tied up in the rot, and I wanted to get far away from the decay and far away from him.

We had been over this a thousand times now, and usually, Dr Steinberg would let me vent about Tom and simply nod, letting me air my angry thoughts out loud instead of where they normally screamed silently, like battering birds against my rib cage. She didn't contradict or agree or blame or even suggest. She simply acknowledged my feelings, and that was enough.

Only today, she had something else to say.

"Do you think Tom hides his grief to protect *you*?" Dr Steinberg asked casually.

My hackles go up, and my defences twitch at her disloyal allegiance with him.

"He isn't *protecting* me. He's carried on, business as usual", I say bitterly, gazing out of the window at the retreating suits heading back to work.

"Grief presents itself in many ways, Kate". Dr Steinberg stops writing.

“You think I’m punishing him by sleeping with somebody else?” I say a little sharply

“Or perhaps punishing yourself,” she replies kindly.

We sit in silence for a few minutes.

When I walk back into the waiting room, Dominic is waiting, as promised. I’m stiff and a little cold around him as I’m feeling uneasy about Dr Steinberg’s words, and I bristle as he touches my arm. We head out onto the road, and he grabs me more forcibly this time, making me look him in the eye. I begin to calm down and relax enough to let him kiss me.

I stiffen again at the sound of a car screeching way too fast alongside us and off down the leafy road. Anger bubbles inside the pit of my stomach as my mind flashes instinctively back to Connie, lifeless on the road. Dominic immediately pulls me in tighter and shouts aggressively at the black sports car. It’s fine, it’s fine, it’s fine, I tell myself, breathing deeply in and out. It’s nothing… just a stupid woman driving too fast.

I was restless that night, more restless than usual. The room is stuffy, even with the windows open, and I toss and turn, throwing my pillow onto the floor.

Tonight, it isn’t just Connie who keeps me awake but also Tom. Dr Steinberg’s words seep into my brain, and for the first time in a very long time, I take a long, hard look at Tom.

I turn restlessly as I contemplate the doctor's words. Yes… grief presents itself in different ways. Grief isn't sexy. Grief is angry and ugly; it's lonely and hidden.

CHAPTER 18

DOMINIC

Wednesday

I gaze down at the morning runners pounding through the curves and folds of Hyde Park below Dr Steinberg's room. I haven't been back here in almost a year, not since Helena booked me those six sessions. Today, I'm hanging around for Kate…back in the waiting room where we first met.

My mind drifts back to those heavy sessions with Dr Steinberg…not my cup of tea at all, and I feel twitchy even just being here.

Dr Steinberg had that annoying way of not really saying much and yet still prizing info out of you. My worst nightmare of a woman. I ended up telling her more about myself than I had told anyone in my life.

They are manipulative fuckers; these shrinks, when you think about it.

Helena had been the most energetic girl in the room when we first met at a house party in Fulham. Twenty-one years ago, to be precise. She was beautiful, no doubt about it, but no more beautiful than half a dozen other girls that were there that night. What set her apart by a mile was her energy. She laughed louder than anyone in the room and smiled with her eyes as well as that lovely pouty mouth. She tipped beer after beer into her and greedily ate the pizza like it was her last, dying meal. She looked hungry for food, drinks, cigarettes, and life. She couldn't get enough of me, and for a long time, things were great.

Helena was working for a beauty magazine at the time. Pretty much working for free as you did back then if you wanted to get a foot on the ladder.

A first-class degree in English Literature wasn't enough to secure a permanent junior role, even with the crappiest of pay. Only a well-connected family friend could secure that. Helena had no such family friend, coming from an intellectual family of scientist geeks. Unfeasibly bright and comfortable in their large but dilapidated house in Oxford, they had no connections or affinity to the glamorous world of beauty.

Helena working for nothing for almost two years. She wrote endless articles and features, researched day and night and began using her family's scientific background to her advantage as she started to speak up loudly about the science behind make-up and skin care. She talked of hydration, collagen and anti-ageing ingredients long before they became big business and big money.

She loved her job and had risen through the ranks to become beauty editor on a large publication, but I had told her she did not need to go back to work after having our first daughter. Luckily for her, I was already earning a ridiculous amount of money by then.

In hindsight, I should have made her go back... she got lazy and, with too much time on her hands, started to second guess where I was every five minutes until, in the end, I had to lie about where I was just for a quiet life.

I wasn't sure how Dr Steinberg would react to me confessing to having one-night stands or short flings. She would assume I was an asshole, or maybe she would wonder what I was like in bed... maybe she thought both, but she didn't say. I didn't mention Kate to her as that only started half way through my sessions, and luckily I haven't been back since.

Kate and I don't usually meet at her counselling... but today, I suggested we grab some breakfast afterwards as I happen to have a meeting close by. We head out of the building, and I pull her in for a kiss; I can see she's had a tough session. We're interrupted by the angry screech of wheels, and as I look up, I see the offending black sports car flying out of a parking space and racing down the quiet, residential road. A flash of black metal and blonde hair follow the piercing noise before it finally disappears from sight.

"Stupid Bitch!!" I shout at the back of the car, mainly for Kate's benefit. I know she'll be furious with such reckless driving after Connie, and I don't want her in a bad mood over breakfast.

CHAPTER 19

TEDDY

Friday

I'm at the hotel super early, but I've tons of emails to catch up on and lots on my mind since my call with Seb.

I sit at a table in the restaurant of the Huxley and order a double gin and tonic. It's too early to be drinking, not even five yet, but I need it. It feels longer than two days since Amanda and I were here, but with no real sleep since then, every day has felt like ten. I'm too wired to sleep.

"Bad day Mr V?" Rico places the G&T down in front of me and gives my shoulder a friendly pat. I try to re arrange my tortured face into a bright smile.

"Oh, you know... usual office politics. I should quit and just work here with you, Rico...looks much more fun. I make a pretty mean margarita as it happens... give you youngsters a run for your money' I force a laugh.

"Well, if it makes you feel any better... it takes us youngsters two hours of working in here just to pay for one of your G&Ts... PLUS... I don't have a girlfriend nearly as beautiful as yours. Cheer up man...life is good". He laughs and points his finger and thumb at me like a gun... winking as he saunters back to the bar, not a penny in his pocket or a care in the world.

If only, I think...if only.

My 'beautiful girlfriend' is practically a stranger who only meets me because I pay her, and I can't afford these G&Ts either...I'm up to my eyes in shit.

"So, what happened with you and your wife then?" Amanda quizzed me on Wednesday night after my amazing massage.

She lit up one of her fancy cigarettes and blew it straight into my face.

"She got fed up of me always working or travelling," I said truthfully, taking the cigarette from her mouth and dragging deeply on it.

I blew an impressive smoke ring towards the high ceiling of the hotel. A trick I perfected back at Uni to impress my then-girlfriend.

“So she was banging someone else then.” She states this as fact.

“Nooooo, she’s not like that. She’s a good woman, a good wife.” I searched for the right way to describe lovely Suzie.

“Ted…(everyone’s) like *that*”, she looked at me with a hint of pity at my evident naivety.

“No, you’re wrong. She begged for me to be more “present,” as she put it. Wanky word if you ask me…but I didn’t want to slow down. It’s not that I didn’t want to be with *them*… it’s just, I love my work, you know… and I’m good at it. I never for one-minute thought she would ask me to leave. Never.

“Did you fight for her?” She had propped herself up on one elbow, allowing me to admire the curve of her naked hip as it arched in towards me. A move she had no doubt perfected a billion times but needless to say, it worked, and I immediately felt the old fella stirring again at the sight of her perfect body.

“I really did fight. I begged, pleaded, got on my knees and cried. I offered to hand in my notice there and then… but it was too late. She’d made up her mind by then, already seen a solicitor …that really pissed me off actually, out of everything.” My semi hard-on bows down in defeat as I recall the sickening feeling of that awful day. The searing realisation hit the pit of my stomach like a freight train when it sank in that I’d just let the most important things in my life walk right out. I physically threw up.

"Yeah, she was definitely screwing someone else" Amanda's posh voice had cut through my reverie as she yawned, bored of my maudlin and stretched out her naked limbs, languishing like a contented cat.

I pummelled her with the pillow.

"Bitch!"

We laughed easily, like boyfriend and girlfriend. It never felt sordid or weird with her.

"So, what's your game plan?" she demanded, throwing the pillow down behind her and sprawling back on the bed. Arms outstretched above her head, white blonde hair spread over the pillow and long, toned legs slightly splayed and hanging just over the edge of the bed. Relaxed and shameless, I remember thinking to myself with a smirk of admiration.

I knew she was only extending her time to increase her pay with these silly little questions, but frankly, I didn't care; I wanted the company.

"I mean, are you hoping to win Suzie back, or are you just going to screw hookers for evermore and stay married to your job?"

"I don't screw hooker (s)…I screw you," I retorted, leaning over and topping up our glasses with more chilled wine. She barely touched hers.

"So, maybe you should think about putting me up in a nice little flat instead? It must cost you a fortune booking this hotel twice a week."

I had roared with laughter at her audacity.

"I don't have as much money as you seem to think I have. I pay for a house for my wife, a flat for myself and now an apartment for my…who are you again? My?

"Whore?" she confirmed with a smile, taking the tiniest sip of wine as if it were poison or piss.

"I was going to say…lover." I had looked at her meaningfully. The memory now makes me cringe as I sip my gin and tonic in the restaurant. Cringe because she had looked utterly horrified.

"Ted. I really should get going, you know. It's getting late, and I'm sure you have an early start, seeing your kids and all." she had put down her almost full glass of wine and swung her long legs off the side of the bed.

"You could stay the night?" I had suggested, even though I could tell I'd already freaked her out with the 'L' word.

She ignored me and jumped into the shower…

I stayed in bed. I'd paid for the night, so I had no intention of going back to my lonely, man flat. I grabbed my laptop and read through some work emails while I waited for her to shower and dress.

And there it was. It caught my attention as soon as I had skimmed my inbox. The nameless email address:

From: viewer@hotmail.co.uk

To: Tedvillandry@cmw.com

Subject: I.O.U
Hello Ted.
Still skimming the cream, I see.
£100k by next Friday, and we don't tell the big boss.
Kindest Regards,
An old friend

Was this some sick kind of joke?

"Ok, Teddy, I'm going", Amanda had called, fastening up her coat, tying the belt tightly, and lifting the collar high before she slowly gathered the notes I left for her on the dressing table and popped them into her leather tote.

"You ok, Ted?" she had cocked her head to one side, looking at my ashen face.

"Huuuuuhhhh, mmm, yeah, yeah, I'm good. I'll see you next Wednesday, and hey.... thank you."

"See you Wednesday" She winked and blew a little kiss as she threw her bag over one shoulder.

I had re-read the email six or seven more times after she left, searching for something familiar, someone familiar. My heart was racing, and my mouth was bone dry. Was this a hoax, or had somebody found out what I had been up to? Was this Seb? Or another colleague or one of the actual clients. No, nobody could possibly have known. I hadn't mentioned to Suzie that I was struggling to pay for both properties. I didn't drunkenly brag or confess to an old mate that I had 'borrowed' a little extra from a few clients. I hadn't left any paper trail. No. I had told no one; I was certain of that.

I had received three more emails since that first one last Friday. Each one was more sinister than the last. This didn't seem Seb's style, and Charles hadn't mentioned any problem with him or his account since the two of them had their private lunch.

Maybe I had it wrong? Either way, I didn't have the kind of money this person wanted. Yes, I had been skimming, but there wasn't a wad of notes under my mattress; it got eaten up pretty quickly with my outgoings. It's expensive paying for two homes, college fees and a twice-weekly session at a nice hotel with my…whore.

I'd been normalising my time with Amanda for so long but saying the word out loud made me feel like a dirty old man. I wondered if this bastard knew about her too. The thought was nauseating. Even though we were no longer together, Suzie would be horrified and embarrassed. The kids would write me off. They might forgive me for money laundering, but certainly not for sleeping with a prostitute.

I had barely slept a wink since Friday, but I was still looking forward to seeing Amanda tonight to escape the madness and have some company. It was coming up to 5.30 pm, she would be here in three hours or so, and we could relax, switch off and forget it all. I took a slug of gin and tonic. For now, I needed to focus and go through all of my trash and junk, every single email sent, and then change every password and figure out what the fuck was going on here.

My phone buzzed, and Amanda's name flashed up.

WhatsApp:

"Ted, I'm so sorry, but I can't make it tonight…I'm really unwell and need to stay in bed. How about Tomorrow instead?"

Fuck's sake!!! Another waste of money and even more debt.

My chest tightened.

JASON

Wednesday

"Jason hung around the door between the stairwell and the restaurant bar to get a good look at Teddy V,

drinking himself into oblivion, the dirty lush. He could put it away that one. Not content with ordering bottle after bottle for him and his tart, he regularly packed away a fair few alone in the bar first for his warm - up act.

'Drinking alone…the road to ruin, Jason.' his Mum used to say as she was sipping on her nightly sherry.

I'm surprised this piss head could still get it up after the cargo he sank. Maybe he couldn't, I thought with a cackle. Maybe that's why he hired prozzies, to revive his drunken dick before it fell over and passed out on parade.

There were a few other familiar faces in here tonight, but nothing wildly exciting was going down, so he went back for a quick eyeful of swimmer's tits before making his way back to the security office and clicking the cameras back on."

CHAPTER 20

AMANDA

Wednesday

That was not his wife. The woman outside the therapist's office was not Dominic's wife. The woman was tall and blonde, like me… not dark and petite, like his wife!

I'd seen a picture of Helena Box on Facebook some time ago, I couldn't remember her face clearly, but I remember she wasn't tall OR blonde. It absolutely wasn't her. I was shaking and sick with jealousy as I flew out of my parking space in Marylebone and raced past them, driving as fast as I could from the pair of them.

I wanted to be sick. It was insane, but it felt as though he had cheated on *me* and not his wife. I shook with anger. He had cheated on me many times when we were first together, although he always denied it. He had a girl in his actual bed once, but it turned out she was just a friend; nothing happened, and both fell asleep drunk. He was so furious at my accusations that in the end, I think I made him cheat…but I was different now; I wouldn't be as clingy or demanding. I just needed a second chance.

The boring wife of twenty years was one thing, but if he was in the first flush of lust or, god forbid, love with somebody new and exciting… that was a much bigger obstacle to navigate.

I drove straight to an old restaurant bar, where I used to hang out a million years ago and ordered myself a vodka tonic, despite it being the morning. My hands shook as I took out my phone and texted the devil himself…Jimmy.

"Jimmy, I'll get the money for you as soon as I can…I promise I'm working on it. I could really use a hit right now…for old time's sake. Could you meet me at Darcy's off Great Portland Street? Mandy".

I knew it was stupid, having been clean for so long and also the terror of Jimmy all these weeks hounding me and threatening me… but maybe I needed to get him back on my side, keep your friends close and your enemies closer, it would hopefully calm him down a little if I played nice. I was getting desperate, and maybe the best option was to bide myself some time with him.

Jimmy didn't bother replying. He simply turned up. Appearing so quickly that I wondered if he already knew where I was. He didn't touch the stuff himself but handed over the small bag indiscreetly and stayed just long enough to remind me of my much bigger debt.

"Don't worry about this one, babe; this one's on the house, a little treat from me," He said with a wink. "Just make sure you get the rest of the money to me by next week, and then we're good. That's my girl."

I drove home, collecting a bottle of grey goose on my way, parked up my BMW and opened the wrap of coke as soon as I was inside the flat. I didn't bother with a mixer for the vodka or even a glass; I drank neat from the bottle as I racked up line after line, flicking through pictures of Dominic, Helena and their kids on Facebook.

I stared hard at the screen and then zoomed in on her again. OMG.

"OH MY GOD", My voice echoed around the empty kitchen as I clicked onto her face.

I knew the woman at my gym looked familiar. HELENA BOX. It was her! His WIFE, the one who splashed me. She looked different with make up on and her hair down, but it was definitely her. Dominic's wife... in MY gym, not their swanky health club. Why?

I hadn't paid enough attention to *her* pictures before, always too busy gazing at him … but, yes, it was definitely the same woman that splashed me. I clamped my hand over my mouth in shock.

My brain was racing, assisted by the white powder. My god, his wife must be following *me*. Why?

I was following her husband, and she was following me? She must have cottoned on to his cheating. By following him, she had been led to me…the unintentional red herring. This was nuts. I took a big slug of vodka from the bottle.

I was wired but still aware that I had to meet Teddy in around six hours. I needed to pull myself together. I folded the remaining gear, keeping a line or two for later to see me through the night. I was bound to crash after this morning's madness.

I ran a bath and eased myself into the soapy water, trying to clean the dirt that was inside my body rather than outside. As the coke started to wear off, the self -hatred began to kick in already.

I hated myself for being so weak. One set back, and I'd undone years of good work. I closed my eyes and tried to think of good things, normal things. The only good thing I had in my life was Teddy.

Ted was such a decent guy, still boyish, for a man in his forties. Stocky but toned, lightly tanned, with a thick head of dirty blonde hair. He was wonderful company, and the conversation always flowed. He treated me better than anyone.

I roll the word "lover" around on my tongue as I lather my limbs with a new apricot scrub. It had irritated me to hear Teddy refer to me like that. He was getting far too attached. A hazard of the job, and the agency insists that we notify them if this happens. They will then swap you for a new girl and break any bonds. I haven't mentioned it to them… I can't afford to lose Ted's twice-weekly booking, and actually, I don't want to. In another life, I could like him.

My parents would love him. I often pictured them back in our beautiful home in Sussex.

It had the most wonderful garden that ran wild around the entire house. The woodland rose grandly like a castle wall around our home before falling softly down to the magical Lavender spring below. The spring was a revered place of natural beauty and attracted endless families for walks and picnics along the bank. Hordes of visitors would head to the spring on their bank holidays and warm weekends. My siblings and I would climb the oak tree nearest to the water and watch them from a distance. They followed their maps and camped on tartan blankets with delicious hampers before taking endless pictures of their kids against the backdrop of the stunning freshwater spring.

We had no need to wait for bank holidays. It was our home and our spring.

As children, Florence, my younger sister and Alice, my twin, would hide from our older brother, Ben… racing through the woodland and laying dead in the reeds until eventually, frustrated, we would give up and find him casually smoking a spliff under a tree. He hadn't bothered to look for us at all.

Ben would dare Alice and I to steal sandwiches from the visitor's hampers whilst they turned their backs to take pictures. Sometimes we were chased by an angry father, but he would never catch us as we knew the woodland like the back of our hand, and we would race like the wind, squealing with delight and tossing the stolen sandwiches into the air.

My heart aches a little as I think of Ben. Ben took his own life at seventeen. Nearly four years older than Alice and I, he had always seemed the happiest boy alive. He had tons of friends and a pretty girlfriend, so it was incomprehensible. He hadn't even left a note. It crucified us all, and I'm ashamed to say that his funeral was where I first tried cocaine. I was thirteen and innocent in this world, but that day, I wanted to escape, and Ben's best friend, Dominic, had provided just that in a tiny white line. I was hooked from the first hit. Hooked on the coke and hooked on Dominic.

I pull the plug in the bath, shaking the old memories away. I'm clearly on a comedown, I can tell…my mind is nostalgic and maudlin, and I'm desperate for another line to pick me back up.

I have another few hours until I need to be at The Huxley. I sigh as I see yet another message from Jimmy.

I had spent ten hard weeks in rehab to get clean, which cost an arm and a leg, but it drummed into me the importance of going cold turkey, not just on the drugs but also on anyone associated. I had changed my phone, address, and social habits. I was lucky; I had the money to clean up and had my own place to live. The regular, good money from escorting allowed me to save myself when no one else could.

I'm careful. I insist on condoms (always). I had the coil fitted for extra safety and still get tested every other month. No chances.

I work for a glossy "agency", not some slimy pimp that you see on an ITV drama.

I sit down and hug the towel around my body before re-reading Jimmy's last message.

Jimmy S

Online

17:28

"Good to see you, Mandy. Look forward to receiving the cash next week, babe."

I locate Teddy's number and cancel him immediately. There's no way I can see him tonight. I suggest tomorrow night instead, which is risky as it's Dom's regular night, but now I know he isn't there with his wife; I'm past caring. Let her follow us both there.

CHAPTER 21

KATE

Tonight, I'm meeting him again in the hotel restaurant at eight-thirty and as usual, my stomach is lurching. I'm running late, so I take an Uber all the way from my house to The Huxley, which is a little excessive but needs must. When I arrive, I scan the small restaurant urgently, checking first that there is no one I know, before sitting at the table in the far corner.

He follows a few minutes behind and does the same sweep of the restaurant/bar before joining me at the table.

"God, you won't believe the day I've had," he says, grabbing my hands over the menu and throwing himself into his seat.

I can't help but smile, even though I am still feeling anxious.

"Yeah, I've had a similar day; Freddie went.."

"Red or white?" he interrupts.

"Erm…red, please. Yeah, I was saying Freddie went to a meeting today for siblings who…."

"Are we eating, or shall we just head to the room?" he says with a lascivious wink.

He always cuts straight to the chase, and it's heady.

"You look very sexy", He breathes.

"Let's fuck and eat later" I surprise myself with my bold crassness, but I'm edgy and upset, and I can't relax or stop tapping my foot. I need a physical release.

He's out of his chair and leading me out of the restaurant and back to the lift before I can change my mind. Not that I will.

The lift door closes, and at the first hint of privacy, he pushes me back against the wall, both hands roughly pushing my breasts up at the same time as he kisses me hungrily. He separates my legs with his knee and pushes his self against me so that I can feel him, hard and strong, through the fabric of his jeans. The lift beeps to open, and he pulls away quickly and marches straight out as I follow like a dishevelled puppy, pulling and smoothing at my dress as I nod politely at a guy with a weird moustache, waiting to enter our lift. Luckily, he is too busy checking his phone and barely raises an eyebrow as he brushes past me.

I head through the door to our room, dropping my coat and bag and turning urgently, reaching for his mouth. His hands are in my hair, and we kiss aggressively, our bodies pressed tight, ripping at each other's clothes, until I drop to my knees, unbuckling him eagerly. I take him in my mouth and groan as I slide my warm mouth over his long cock, slowly easing him in and out as I let him fuck my wet mouth.

We fuck on and off for hours, as is our way until he whispers "enough," and we lay still like tight spoons.

Later we swim in the huge, clear fish tank, facing each other from opposite sides. He takes a sip of red wine, swims a couple of strokes over to my side and rises from the water, smoothing back his wet, dark hair. He looks incredible, and my breath catches in my throat. I'm starting to need him too much.

The cold, hard layer protecting my broken heart is starting to melt, and it is terrifying.

"You know, we should talk about moving this forward, Kate. This isn't fair on anyone," he says, lifting my leg up high out of the water and sucking softly on my big toe. My stomach flips again.

"Really?????" I say, closing my eyes and resting my head on the back of the pool.

I don't want to think about anything. I don't want to think about Tom, our son or family or friends. I don't want to think about all the lying, the destruction for so many people. I don't want to think about Connie. I want to think of nothing. It's selfish to the core, but I need the escape.

I sip my wine and float away for just a few seconds. Peace is mine for now, at least.

I feel a soft kiss on my forehead and a spray of hot water as he climbs out and leaves me to float.

I have to take the Eurostar in the morning as we have our first international booking for The Pink Pig in Paris. It's a small event for twenty people, and we will barely break even, but it's wonderful to have a booking out of the UK. It would have been easier to stay in a hotel closer to Kings X, but this is our place, and it's beginning to feel like our home from home, which is worrying, to say the least.

We are starting to recognise a few regular visitors at the hotel now, and certainly, the staff know us well. Dom must be their best customer, booking every Thursday night plus any extra nights or afternoons we can snatch. He always insists on paying despite my offers. I don't often stay the whole night, but sometimes it's possible. Becoming a familiar face around the hotel was definitely worrying, but as Dom had pointed out, they knew nothing of our story, and we knew nothing of theirs.

"Are you hungry" He calls out.

"Ravenous", I reply.

"Good. I'm ordering room service; then we can watch a movie in bed."

It sounded so normal. Like an ordinary couple in love and yet…I can't go there.

I lay my head on the water to drown out the pulsing din in my ears. Breathing in and out slowly, just as Dr Steinberg showed me.

JASON

Thursday

> *"They must have been going at it hammer and tongue again by the looks of all that food, heading up to his room, Jason thinks. Silver tray after silver tray, enough for ten people and another bottle of plonk. Smarmy bastard. The CCTV picks him up, answering the door in his white robe with his dark, wet hair. Dominic Box, Casa-fuckin-nova, he lets the bellboy in with the trolley, and Jason zooms out, bored but irritated.*
>
> *Flicking onto camera seven, he watches Ted, guzzling alone at the bar, waiting for his tart. It was unusual. These two were in on the same night as they both only ever booked the fancy suite. Looked like Dominic Box had got in first and bagged the best room. I almost felt*

sorry for Teddy. I hated both of them, but Teddy was marginally more likeable. Jason took his notebook and pen out of the drawer to jot down the movements of tonight's guests. He was feeling the same old anger and disappointment swilling around in him."

CHAPTER 22

DOMINIC

Thursday

The Iris café had been heaving this lunchtime when I met Will to discuss the idea of potentially divorcing. Full of local suits and workers, all attracted by the delicious, Italian artisan food which was served up by two pretty Italian girls and their loud, charismatic father, with his cumbersome, white moustache and extended tummy. A little piece of Sicily right here in dusty Holborn.

Will is already seated and thumbing through a copy of the metro when I weave through the tables to join him. He's sipping his coffee and eyeing up the waitress instead of the actual pages before him. He's still a handsome bastard. Always was.

He jumps up to greet me, patting my back, and I mirror my good friend and do the same back.

"Mate, how's it going?" he asks enthusiastically, eyes bright, as he plonks himself back down, thrusting a small menu toward me. "I don't have ages, I'm afraid, back in court at one thirty, sorry."

"No need to apologize", I say, "let's order quickly".

We tuck into a hearty dish of homemade beef ragu...with fresh basil and Parmesan.

"That is seriously the best Italian I have ever eaten," Will says with pleasure. "Well…apart from Maria Romano, on that trip to Naples in 96'," he adds with a lascivious wink and a deep laugh.

Amazing how within two minutes, we revert back to two eighteen-year-old lads on a rugby tour, nudging, winking, wrestling and laughing at our own stupid jokes. Sport, girls, beer, and music…it was so easy back then.

"Sweet Marie…she had as much hair downstairs as she did on her head." He laughs loudly, shaking his head at the distant memory, whilst cramming another large mouthful of rich meat sauce into his still laughing mouth. "Still…Italians do it better. Anyway, come on… what's up, Dom? You said you wanted advice, and I take it you mean the legal kind and not my expert advice on women."

"Hmmm, a bit of both, really," I say, raising my eyebrow.

"Oh, Christ, mate. You aren't dipping your stoke into the home fires are you… that hot little au pair of yours?"

"NOOOOOO. I'm not dipping anything into anything,' I lie. " I'm just talking about me and Helena. We aren't getting along, haven't for a long time, to be honest, and I just… I don't know…I thought it might be wise to see what the situation would be "IF" we chose to separate.

"Mate, you must be pretty far down the line to be asking this kind of advice. That sounds like more than just not getting along. I thought you two were rock solid. I'm really sorry to hear that. So, there isn't someone else then?" He eyeballs me over his next mouthful.

"No. Nobody else. We just don't have that much in common anymore. We've been together a long time… you know how it is. Listen, don't mention it to Simone, please. I know her and Helena occasionally talk."

"No, of course not. Look, I have to get back to work, but I'll drop you an email this afternoon outlining the usual course of action and the probable outcome. You can kiss goodbye to half of your cash though (at the very least)…so I would think long and hard before doing anything rash. Right, I've got to shoot. Speak soon mate and look after yourself."

We stand again for a goodbye back pat, and he stalks off out of the restaurant knowing full well I am lying through my teeth.

Will was as good as his word and emailed me a few hours later with an outline of steps to take when considering divorce. There was a long list of implications to consider. It was necessary to list at least six or seven reasons why you were asking your spouse for a divorce. Six terrible reasons or points of blame are to be cited. It would be better if I could somehow persuade her to divorce me…that way, I wouldn't look like a shit to the kids, and also, she might not take me to the cleaners. The financial implications were mind-boggling. It was a wonder anyone ever divorced. I save Will's email for another day and head to the gents for a quick freshen before I head to The Huxley.

We meet in the restaurant, and unusually she is there before me and already seated at a table in the far corner, out of sight. The waiting staff must have a field day speculating about her and I and our set up, what with our shady behaviour, always hidden away in a dark corner, week after week. I can see that Kate is restless and twitchy the minute I sit down, but I haven't got the energy to get into it after my conversation with Will…I'm too busy thinking about all the money I am going to lose just to get away from her nagging. I'm taken aback but delighted by her immediate suggestion to head upstairs and screw each other's brains out. I need no persuasion, obviously, and we flee to the room to do exactly that.

The physical desire is as strong as ever, week after week and month after month.

We lay in the large bed, wrapped in their wonderfully crisp white sheets. There is something so good about fucking in white sheets, and I lay smiling like a Cheshire cat, my arms above my head, happy and satisfied but starving after our work out.

I fill the bath…or tank, as it's known. More hot water and a little oil before pouring us both a glass of wine as we take a leisurely soak together.

"When we live together, we'll have to have a huge bath. That is my one and only request." I say, wincing as her foot accidentally kicks my balls from under the water as I swim in closer to her.

"Whooooa, once step at a time." She says, rather annoyingly refusing to humour me with fantasy talk about where we will live and what we will do and the holidays we will take. This only excites me more, chasing her.

We sip our wine in silence and lay in the bath until the water begins to cool.

"Are you hungry?" I ask her as I step out and towel myself dry.

"Ravenous," she says, and I raise my eyebrows with a smirk and head off to dial in our room service order.

I take the tray off the bellboy at the door; I don't want him perving at Kate, who is still soaking in the tub, topping it up with more hot water every few minutes. I'm feeling in need of another drink. Her evasiveness has bothered me more than I would like to admit. She should be delighted I'm even contemplating leaving my wife for her. I swallow my irritation and focus on the young guy.

"That's great, thanks, mate. Smells delicious," I say, slipping the young lad a £20 and peering in on Kate as I close the door behind him.

"Would madam care to join me for dinner?" I ask.

I stare at her as she climbs out of the tank to dry off. I love the sight of her. Her body is how a woman should be. It's lean and fit, yet curvy and soft in all the right places.

"I'm getting horny again; hurry up and cover yourself with a robe before I bend you over and give you a good seeing to."

She smiles almost shyly. God knows why; I know every inch of her, inside and out, but it's endearing all the same and a change from some of the brazen tarts I have been with…always off-putting in the end. Men like to hunt their game…not be spoon-fed the deer from the comfort of their own bed.

I serve dinner, which is delicious and another one of the attractions of the hotel. We share blackened cod, baked in a crisp, sweet banana leaf with a cauliflower puree and sweet potatoes, drizzled with harissa and chilli flakes. I pour more wine for us into new, large glasses and join her at the small table.

We eat in silence at first. I want to ask more about Tom, about us, but I don't want to be a buzz kill either, so I eat hungrily and enjoy the taste of the Argentinian wine.

"This is soooo good," she says between mouthfuls.

"The food or us?" I raise an eyebrow. I can't resist pushing it.

"Both", she smiles, and I clink her glass.

"I'm not going to ask you anything else tonight, but you can't hide away forever, Kate" I push my empty plate away and stretch out my legs.

She throws her head back and laughs, a huge and hearty laugh, with tears in her eyes.

I slam my glass down a little harder than intended; I'm getting a little pissed off with her attitude.

"Noooo, no. I'm not laughing at what you said; I'm not laughing at us. I'm mwhahahahaha."

She points at my crotch, and I look down.

"I can see your dick whilst I'm eating", she bursts. "THAT'S what needs to hide away!"

I look down, and we both laugh as I re-tighten my robe.

"Right, that's it…over my knee you go," I say, grabbing her by the belt of her robe and pulling her onto my lap and my growing hard-on.

JASON

Thursday

"Jason flicks across to screen twenty-three. He rarely paid much attention to the "newbies" unless a particularly tasty sort came in. He preferred to keep tabs on the "regulars" at the hotel. They could give East Enders a run for their money, this shower of shit. There was nothing he hadn't seen going on under this roof in the last few years. Stuff to make your hair curl. Old Teddy V was back in for the night, looking like he had the weight of the world on his shoulders and ordering drink after drink at the bar.

Jason lit up another rolly, ignoring the no-smoking sign. Teddy's escort had arrived in the foyer and had been smiling at Joseph like she was the Queen of Sheba. He zoomed in on screen six as she waltzed into the lift. He couldn't believe this bird, always marching along, her nose in the air, thinking she was something special.

'Fur coat and no knickers' as his mum used to say. He would love to grab the stuck-up bitch and ask her how much she charged in front of all the hotel guests. Maybe one of these days, I might even book her for myself. Jason let out a cackle at the thought before pressing the pause button on a close-up of her smug face.

"Anything exciting happening in the bar tonight, Stevo?" He was feeling unusually jovial. Steve rarely looked at anything other than the foyer, so Jason was pleasantly surprised to see the nosey bastard taking a peek in the bar. Maybe he wasn't such a boring prick after all. If he bucked his ideas up, he might even tell him about the stairwell route around the back of the bedroom corridors. Who knew a bit of teamwork could benefit them both? You scratch my back, and I'll scratch yours. You switch off my CCTV camera, and I'll switch off yours. He chuckled at this new plan. They thought he was stupid in this place; little did they know, he was three steps ahead of the bleeding lot of them."

CHAPTER 23

TEDDY

Thursday

We don't usually meet on a Thursday, but as Amanda had cancelled our usual slot last night, I agreed on tonight instead. Another massive bill for me, having already paid for last night's room. My heart was racing more and more by the day as the debts mounted further and further out of control.

Amanda had never cancelled before, so I hadn't made a fuss, but it meant I couldn't secure The Duke of Shoreditch suite tonight, which was already pre-booked by another couple. Still, the other rooms were pretty nice.

I'm early as usual and enjoying my fourth drink at the bar. I notice a good-looking couple leave the restaurant without ordering anything. They look too giddy and besotted by each other to be a married couple. There is an air of naughtiness about them. I wonder if they are here under the same circumstances.

The beautiful, blonde woman looks a little like Amanda; I think to myself with a grin as I watch her leave, his hand on her backside. He, on the other hand, looks nothing like me…a good three inches taller with that dark, swarthy look that women seem to love. I check my watch, almost seven pm. I need to head up to my room; Amanda will be here by eight. I sign my drinks tab with Rico and head to the lobby. I need to freshen up and maybe order some more drinks to wind down. The three gin and tonics have not even touched the sides this afternoon, which is a tad worrying. I need more than a quick livener tonight, though, what with the emails playing heavily on my mind. I have one week to come up with the cash… or else what?

"Good evening Mr.Villandry. How are you, sir?" flaps the beaming maître D, Joseph.

"Evening Joseph" I nod. "Could I grab a bottle of Sauvignon Blanc and two glasses up in my room?" I add hastily as I walk on straight past him and over to the reception desk to pick up my key card.

"Certainly, Sir, I'll have that organised right away", he calls to the back of my head.

I bomb up to the fourth floor in the lift and do a quick dad-jog down the corridor and along to my room.

I burst through the room, thinking I might grab another quick shower before she gets here, but I jolt in surprise as I see Amanda lying on the bed, naked as the day she was born and with a blindfold pulled over her eyes.

"You're late", she murmurs without removing the mask.

It's a wonderful and immediate stress buster, and I yank off my clothes at super speed and join her on the king-sized bed. The sex is great, as always. Fast and furious, Amanda is enthusiastic and moves keenly beneath me to the same frantic rhythm until I can't hold off any longer.

"Wow," I say as I roll off her and lay next to her, my heart pounding heavily in my chest. "I should arrive late more often. What a welcome! You could give a man a heart attack."

"Hmmm, well, I didn't want to waste time; I'm only free for a couple of hours tonight. We still have another hour and fifty-three minutes to err…chat," Amanda arches her eyebrow and lets out a huge hearty laugh.

"Stoooop it… seven minutes? Nooo." I say, wide-eyed and hoping she is winding me up.

"You were late, so it was closer to four" She wipes a tear of laughter from the corner of her eye and slaps my thigh.

I cover my eyes in mock shame and groan.

"Well, it's your fault for looking so damn sexy," I say as I hear a knock at the door. That must be the bellboy with the wine.

"Will you have a glass? A small one won't kill you," I call to her as I head to the bathroom and quickly grab a towel. I open the door and take the wine and glasses from the bellboy without letting him inside. I don't need him tripping over my undies on his way in.

"So, how was your day?" she asks, lighting up a cigarette in the no-smoking room and opening up the sash window. She perches on the ledge, legs crossed, still naked and blowing smoke out onto the City streets below.

I take a large gulp of wine, almost half of my glass.

"Jeeze…bad day?" she says, nodding at my half-empty glass.

"I'm having a couple of work issues, that's all. My head's all over the place this week." I say:

"Want to talk about it?" she cocks her head to one side, and the unusual softness in her face immediately makes me want to share the burden. I need to talk to someone, and there is no one I can tell other than her. I know she doesn't judge or even care what I've done, no matter how wrong.

So, I tell her it's just the same work problems again that I mentioned once before.

It had started as a moment of madness. I hadn't slept for months after the first time I did it and swore I would never, ever risk my job again. Yet months passed, and nobody noticed, and nobody came. I started to sleep soundly again, and very soon, that fear turned into a small bubble of adrenalin that sat just under the surface of my skin, like an itch that couldn't be scratched. It just wouldn't go away. Within three months, I had skimmed a little cash again.

It was very ad hoc initially… no strategy, no set figure. I took only what I could whilst sitting pretty under the radar. Yet before long, I had turned the occasional, chaotic skim into a highly sophisticated betting system, which ran like clockwork across fourteen key accounts. "The system" shaved a nominal amount, barely noticeable to a high roller, yet substantial enough for someone like me. The client would see no pattern or cause for concern, despite my "system" following a very distinct algorithm that should be detectable to me only. Or so I had thought.

Amanda had listened in silence with something teetering on admiration.

"Why did you do it?" She had quizzed, taking a last drag of her cigarette before stubbing it onto the outside of the window and flicking the butt below.

"I needed more cash, simple as that?" I had taken another slug of wine. "I haven't even given that question any thought before. I guess I hadn't wanted to let Suzie know that we weren't quite as well off as she presumed or quite as well off as we ought to be, given the hours I had put in over the years. I already felt like a failure, and I wasn't about to admit to her that all this hard work really had been for nothing. Since the split, it had ramped up a little as I was finding it nigh on impossible to pay for a second property after letting Suzie keep our house. Here I was, paying for two properties, her monthly allowance, the kid's every movement, Suzie's every need, plus an astronomical amount of rent on a tiny, shit-hole flat for myself. Men have it easy? Right.

I explain to Amanda that the little habit I had mentioned to her was playing on my conscience again. I don't add that I am now being blackmailed. It sounds far-fetched and ridiculous. I don't want to say it out loud and make it real.

"I know all about habit's" Amanda stretches out her long limbs in front of her. "I had a pretty bad habit once" She stares boldly at me. "I wasn't stealing, well, not at first. It was the old marching powder. It got pretty bad, I can tell you. I kept taking more and more coke because I was addicted. However, the real issue Teddy, was why did I take it in the first place? Only when you look at the root cause can you find your way out of hell. She climbs down from the window and grabs the room service menu, idly flicking through it.

"Ok, why *did* you take cocaine…the very first time?" I ask in return, trying to keep the shock and judgement out of my voice. Oh, dear god, I'm screwing an ex-addict to top it off. Could this day get any worse?

"My brother killed himself," She says, very matter-of-fact, closing the menu and the conversation with a spank. She looks me straight in the eye. Her chin is tilted up, defensive and challenging, but I don't miss the slight wobble.

"I'm sorry". I reach for her arm, but she's already out of reach and walking to the table, pouring herself another full glass, which is unusual. My hand, instead, caresses the air.

"I did it to escape Teddy. It's usually why most people do bad things, why they end up down the wrong path. We're all escaping from something bad…you just need to figure out what your bad is."

"My bad?" I say, and we both laugh.

"I don't know about you, but I'm starving," She jumps up and heads towards the bathroom. "Order for me, Ted; you know what I like," she adds.

I do know what she likes and how she likes it. I know how she eats far too quickly. Otherwise perfect table manners, but she still eats way too quickly. Another habit picked up from boarding school, I wonder. Fighting another seven hundred girls for the last bread roll will do that to you. I also know how she smells of Pears soap underneath her expensive Tom Ford perfume and lavish body creams. The smell is so old school but amazingly clean. I know how she keeps a low-carb diet and prefers to eat a salad with her fish or steak. No more fighting for bread rolls these days.

I now know that her brother killed himself. I know that Amanda is a cocaine addict in recovery. I know that I wish I didn't know any of it. I know that if this gets out to whoever is blackmailing me, I'm truly fucked.

She doesn't stay too long tonight. Eating her food way too quickly, she showers, dresses, collects her money and leaves. I have paid her for the whole night as usual, more wasted cash, but I don't mention it, as I have too much on my mind and could use the space to clear my head and think. I need to think about who exactly is emailing me and how the hell I'm going to sort this out.

I open my laptop and re-read the latest email:

From: viewer@hotmail.co.uk

To: TedVillandry@cmw.com

Subject: I.O.U

Hello Ted.
Tik Tok, Tik Tok
Time's up, old friend.
Kindest Regards,

JASON

Thursday

"Jason wipes the dribble of ketchup that has fallen from his bacon sandwich and onto the new page of his notebook. Grabbing a pencil, he adds tonight's entry of comings and goings.

Flicking back a page and re-reading Dominic Box's greedy room service order. Jason notes down Teddy V's booze order plus the arrival time of his tramp. Everyone is getting laid. He takes an angry bite and curses as another dollop of ketchup lands on the page.

"FUCKKKKKK", He shouts, stamping the side of his fist straight down onto their smeared, red names.

"What's wrong with you?" Steve barks over from his chair. He has his back to Jason, and his cameras are fixed solely on the foyer and restaurants again. Boring asshole.

"Mind your biz," Jason shouts to him, mouth still full of bacon. There's a hierarchy in here, and Steve should wind his neck in before it's accidentally broken."

CHAPTER 24

AMANDA

Thursday

I don't know why I blurted that out about my brother, it's hugely private, and I hate looking vulnerable and weak in front of anyone. I'm so mad with myself; I know Teddy is getting attached, and telling him about my family is only going to fuel his misguided little crush. He will think we are closer than we are. I'm emotional and clearly on a downer after my relapse yesterday.

I had cancelled Teddy last night in the end; I had been too out of it to meet him. It had been a loooong time since I had touched the stuff, and clearly, I no longer had the same tolerance to it these days. It was risky re-arranging for tonight as I knew this was Dominic's night with his bit on the side, but I was emboldened and careless after seeing him with his other woman. Why shouldn't I bump into him if he wasn't with his actual wife? He should feel more awkward than I would. Plus, if his wife was following me, it made sense that she saw us both arriving at the hotel. The sooner she left him, the better.

I had been worrying all day with the constant hassle from Jimmy. I don't know where he thought I could possibly get hold of money like that on my own. The daily stress was becoming intolerable. Seeing Ted was my only comfort.

I wasn't surprised at his little fess-up a few months ago, stealing a few quid from work. Nobody's whiter than white, as I've learnt the hard way; even nice guys like Ted have their little secrets. We all do. I didn't actually care either way, but once Jimmy started hounding me, I began to wonder if maybe I could ask Ted to loan me the money to pay Jimmy off. If I explained things properly to him. I knew he cared for me; I felt sure he would help if I asked.

After tonight's conversation, it's pretty clear that Teddy has no real cash anyway. Fuck, fuck, fuck. I've got it wrong. I had presumed he had money to burn, the way he books me twice a week, overnight, full pay, whether I stay or not. He owns a huge house with his ex, he has his own flat, and he told me he was stealing, for Christ's sake. How can he have no money? I couldn't stay there with Teddy a minute longer. I needed to get out of this hotel and to be alone, to think. If I couldn't ask Teddy to help me pay Jimmy off, then I needed to think of another plan and fast.

Jimmy had looked and seemed harmless enough when I had first met him all those years ago. He was generally to be found in all the newest clubs and member's bars around Soho and West London. He always wore black jeans, a black shirt and a black leather cap, which hid away his solid, baldhead and gave him a more fun and, dare I say (not to his face) camp look. It was dated and uncool, even back then and paired with his extended, twisted moustache, it gave off a vague whiff of Freddie Mercury. Jimmy was everybody's best friend, rubbing shoulders with all the wealthy bankers, trust fund kids and general hangers-on, along with anyone else who simply looked the part. It was fake but fun, and if you needed a hit of something or other to see you through the night and the following night, then Jimmy was the only dealer you dared go to.

Once you had bought from him, you had unwittingly signed a silent pact, enforcing; A) You only bought from him, no matter how desperate for a fix, *and* B) You ordered weekly from him, whether you needed or wanted that much stuff or not. This unspoken contract sent many a "social user" down a rabbit hole of addiction, as we all had more than we actually wanted. Flout the rule, and at best, you faced social suicide; at worst, you faced an unexplained accident. Everybody seemed to accept these absurd rules without question. We fawned over him like he was a celebrity. He had what we needed, what we eventually couldn't live without.

I shiver coldly at the thought of him being back in my life now. Jimmy was smart; he would generously shower his "friends" in a blizzard of marching powder, throwing it wildly around the club like the White Witch of Narnia. Only it wasn't free, nothing was ever free, and it still isn't free all these years later. There are, of course, unspoken T's & C's attached with people like Jimmy. He had a black book of (I.O.U's) some of which dated back months, even years. There were "favours" to collect.

I had been blind and naïve not to realise that Jimmy had merely been biding his time. Like a sly cat watching a bird, he had waited for me, watching, still and unnoticed. He had crept quietly around my new neighbourhood as I finally cleaned up, keeping a respectful distance. He had watched through the flap, unseen, undetected, as I steadily rebuilt my health and wealth, and now the cat wanted his cream.

I tell Teddy that, going forward, Thursday is a better night for me, instead of our usual Wednesday, and he agrees readily…no doubt thinking of the money he will save from not having The Duke Suite. I'm pissed off with his dire financial situation, and I decide to leave him earlier than planned tonight. I also decide this is not the night to run into Dominic, I feel like shit after yesterday, and I just need to go home. I leave after only fifty minutes, regardless of him paying for the whole night. He doesn't question or complain. He knows I'm out of sorts, having spoken about my brother's death, and he has no reason to think that I would have anything else on my mind.

I glance towards the bar as I exit the lift into the foyer, and that's when I see her. Sat alone, sipping a drink at the bar and looking bereft. Helena Box.

I can't help myself. Part of me wants her to believe that it is *me* that he's upstairs with. Me, that her husband is in love with. If only.

I head over to the bar and call out loudly to the barman, "Rico, when you get a minute…send a bottle of Laurent Perrier up to Mr Box and I in The Duke of Shoreditch, please." He looks confused but agrees politely. I march out of the bar, down the steps of the hotel and into my Uber.

JASON

Thursday

> "*That whore hadn't stayed very long tonight, not even an hour. Jason zoomed in closer on her outline,*

watching as she made her way back down in the lift on camera seven. Either Teddy boy couldn't keep it up, or she was servicing different fellas back to back. The thought excited him. He grabbed his pen and added her latest movements onto a clean page with no ketchup. Jason would love to book in with her himself, but he wouldn't be paying, that's for sure. Eleven quid an hour in this shit hole left no spare cash for that.

He whistles with pleasure, thinking how this was becoming one hell of a dossier here in this notepad. He knew when they arrived, who they met, what they ate…He could pretty much tell you what time these idiots took a shite. The thought made him feel powerful, and he wondered, not for the first time, how he could use this to his advantage."

CHAPTER 25

KATE

Thursday

The last two weeks have stretched out like months, and other than a passing hello at Dr Steinberg's each Wednesday and a million text messages a day, I hadn't had any real contact with Dominic since our last visit to The Huxley. The excitement and adrenalin ripple under my skin all over again. I'm falling hard, and I can't seem to stop it.

"Can I get you anything before I leave? Are you hungry?" I called to Tom, swallowing any guilt and quickly checking how many minutes until my Uber arrives.

I march down the hallway and towards the lounge, where Tom is splayed out, watching the football. He doesn't bother to turn around but grabs another handful of crisps and takes a swig from his bottle of beer…sitting up suddenly and closer to the screen when he senses a possible goal.

"Tom, I asked if you wanted anything. I'm leaving in a few minutes?"

Tom laughs. "Nooooo, you have asked me that three times woman. I'm fine. I'll grab something later with Freddie. Just relax and enjoy your night with the girls; you need it. Goooo, have some fun and no talking to strange men." He walks over, kisses my forehead and then leans over to grab the TV remote from the coffee table and turns up the volume in blissful ignorance.

We have been kinder to each other the last few weeks thanks to the new seed planted by Dr Steinberg. I have felt less angry with Tom, and in turn, he has sensed my calm waters and chosen to be around the house a little more.

I nearly don't go. I nearly cancel the whole thing right then and there. He's such a good man. A good man carrying an unbearable burden in the best way he knows how. I am a cunt. I detest the word, but it's what I am; it's what I've become. As quickly as the guilt comes, I tuck it away into one of the boxes that I simply can't deal with. The lid is closed, and I walk robotically to the door.

"See you tomorrow Tom." I'm gone.

I arrive at the hotel super late, it's almost nine, and I'm an hour late already. Dominic has messaged to tell me to meet him in the bar downstairs. I go to the lobby toilets first and douse some hand towels in water and soap to freshen my fanny, just in case. The hand soap burns, and I immediately regret it and try to splash more water all over myself…covering my clothes in water at the same time. "Fuck's sake", I mutter crossly as I try and dry the crotch of my pants with more hand towels. I reapply some lip balm, brush my hair and head down to the private bar.

I'm pretty surprised to see him sitting there as bold as brass, enjoying a glass of champagne with a woman who doesn't look dissimilar to me. Maybe a little younger or just more groomed, I note with an unfamiliar jealousy.

"Sorry to interrupt," I say coldly. I can't help myself. The trouble with cheating is that you already know you're dating a cheater. A double-edged sword of your own making.

"Oh err… hi Kate," he's clearly uncomfortable and without his usual kiss.

"This is Mimi, my mate's sister. We just ran into each other, so weird??" He widens his eyes and arms before turning back to her.

"Mimi, this is Kate…. a… colleague of mine." I seethe inwardly. My intro is a blatant lie, and so I'm guessing hers is too. The sister of his mate? Bullshit, bullshit.

"I'll meet you upstairs," I say, unsmiling. "Good to meet you," I add insincerely. My face is green with jealousy, anger and every ugly emotion in-between as I stalk off towards the lift.

"Do you often meet your colleague's upstairs?" I hear the cow ask loudly as I walk away.

I expect him to follow me upstairs quickly and explain himself, but to my horror, he stays downstairs for almost another hour.

I sit and stew in the room, and I'm just about ready to leave and boiling with rage by the time he lets himself casually into the room at five past ten.

I explode immediately.

"How fucking rude. Cosy little drink with your 'friend' while your mistress waits upstairs for you. You've got some nerve," I add irrationally.

"You're a piece of work," he says calmly, which infuriates me further.

"I'm leaving Dominic. I don't need this shit," I'm crying and have no idea why or where the tears came from. I never show him any emotion. What the hell is wrong with me? I grab my coat and bag.

"Just stop." He says, grabbing my shoulders.

"That girl is my best friend's sister." He stoops to look me straight in the eye. "Correction 'was' my best friend's sister. Ben died… a very long time ago. It was a bit messy …he er…found me with his girlfriend …you know…together. We were only kids, for Christ's sake… it meant nothing…I mean, of course, I felt guilty, but I didn't think it was that big a deal. He didn't even leave a note…it was awful. Although at least his family didn't hate me. I took care of Mimi for them, which they were grateful for. I haven't seen her for years until tonight."

"Took care of her how?" I ask…hating myself for the suspicion that seeps through my voice.

"Stop it right now…don't you dare accuse me of things you know nothing about. This is what you do…it's mad. I've already got one paranoid wife; I don't need another.

Mimi knows I'm married with kids, and I didn't want to get into what a total bastard I am, having an affair and loving another man's wife. I was surprised to see her here tonight; totally random, but she was leaving when I arrived, so we grabbed a drink. Your little tantrum made sure I *did* have to tell her I'm a bastard… which is why I stayed for another drink. You are acting a little crazy, to be honest…did something happen with Tom?"

"Loving me?" I whisper.

"Yes…of course…I love you," he says.

I push my face into his chest and let the tears finally fall. I'm ugly, I'm red, I'm snotty, I'm heaving, and now I have started, I can't stop.

I cry on and off for what seems like days.

He looks awkward and disappears to get the menu, changing the subject and telling me about some stressful deal at the office. He starts to get angry about the deal, and I forget why I am even crying.

We don't have sex, which is a first; he's too angry about work… nor do we eat or drink that night, but instead, we lay together until I fall asleep. When I wake up, it's almost 2 am, and he is busy on his laptop.

"I love you too, Dominic," I say for the very first time. I realise I mean it, and I can feel it too.

He nods and carries on with his email.

The realisation that I must leave Tom is terrifying and yet a relief… but mostly terrifying. It changes everything. It will turn our world upside down when it still isn't the right way up after what happened to Connie. The enormity of the inevitable sadness yet to come completely overwhelms me, and I sleep again for another fourteen hours straight.

It is not Connie that comes to me in my sleep that night but both Tom and Freddie. I am a whisp of air, like a drawing of a cartoon cyclone. I am spinning and soaring so high, but I want to be on the ground with my family. I try and try to push my weight back down, to force myself to reach the ground, where they are playing in my Father's garden …but I am too light; I cannot push myself down to reach them. I am weightless, flying further and further away. Higher and higher, I float. I feel frightened as they disappear beneath me.

CHAPTER 26

DOMINIC

Thursday

The sight of Mimi throws me off completely. Here, of all places, at The Huxley hotel. I hadn't seen her for about twenty years, since I left Sussex for Leeds Uni. She cried when I left and, and it all got a little dramatic as I recall…her questioning where I was, who I was with, why I hadn't called. I soon immersed myself into student life, freedom, new friends and new girls.

I had seen her a couple of times after leaving… once at Christmas after my first term, where I did shag her again for old times, but typically she went stalker again, so I had to cut ties for her own good… then briefly over the summer holidays two years later, when I came back home to stay with my family we slept together again. After that, I changed my number for both of our sanity.

I had taken Amanda, or Mimi, as we called her back then, under my wing after her brother, Ben, had died. I was pretty messed up myself over it … I actually had nightmares about the look on his face when he had caught me shagging his girlfriend. He had cried…I mean, I knew he was gutted; I felt bad… but we never expected him to kill himself…it was nuts. I can't remember her name…it was so long ago…Sarah or Sara, I think…but we agreed never to tell anyone what Ben had seen, and we never spoke or saw each other again after the funeral. I felt pretty cut up; Ben had been my best friend since we were four and the one who had seen me through my own struggles at age ten when my Father left, never to be seen again. I couldn't believe he would do that to his family, to his mates.

Ben, myself and our friends had tried a little coke once or twice before and smoked a few spliff's in the park with some girls from school, but nothing too heavy. After Ben took his own life, I had started to take it more and more regularly. It never got out of hand; it was a teenage phase, but I had let Mimi hang around with us as it made her feel closer to her brother. I allowed her to try a little of the coke herself at his funeral, as she was so distraught, but she was too nuts to handle it and became a bit of a handful after that. She caused me a lot of stress thinking back.

I heard on the grapevine that she got pretty heavily into drugs over those next few years and had eventually been kicked out of home.

Helena and I later re located to New York for a good ten years with my work, and I hadn't given her much thought after that. I hadn't realised just how alike her and Kate were until seeing Mimi here tonight. Seeing her as an adult, a woman, had thrown me and thinking about it, maybe that's exactly why Kate had seemed so familiar to me from the off… in Dr Steinberg's office. She was Mimi's double.

I didn't feel the need to go into the full details with Kate. Our romance had been innocent and a long time ago, and she was angry at seeing me even talking with her. It was pointless to mention. I didn't lie, she *was* my best friend's sister, but that wasn't the whole story.

It had been great to chat with Mimi again tonight. She looked better than I remembered and was doing well, which was great to see. No sign of the rumoured drugs or bad lifestyle of old. She looked sexy. She was working in sales now and told me she had just had a meeting with one of her clients at the restaurant here before spotting me at the bar. I didn't enjoy having to tell her about my complicated home life or about Kate; it wasn't appropriate. Mimi was practically a stranger to me these days, but Kate's little strop had left me with no other choice than to come clean. It was pretty obvious to Mimi what was going on after Kate rudely flounced off.

I hadn't expected the tears or outburst from Kate when I came back up to our room, but Kate had totally lost it, shouting, rambling and crying. I let her sleep it off and sent Mimi a quick message to apologise for Kate's crazy behaviour and suggested a drink one night to smooth things over.

JASON

Thursday

> *"Jason is buzzing tonight. An unexpected little hook-up between Dominic Box and the whore that old Teddy V uses. He scribbled down the new entry. He very much doubted that these two were old pals, so Box must have cottoned on quickly that she was a call girl and decided to tap her up for business. Not enough that he was shagging that other bird here every Thursday, but he was now drinking with the other mush's girl in the same bar! Jason laughed out loud at the audacity of this asshole. His bird looked like she was going to flip her lid when she arrived and saw them at the bar together. This could all get very tasty.*

"Steve, click off the cameras on floors three and four pal. I'm going to take you on a little private tour of the joint."

"Private tour where?" The dozy bastard asks, with his mouth half open.

"Ask no questions, and I'll tell you no lies" He puts a stop to Steve's waffling. Christ, He was regretting the suggestion already. Steve was like an old woman sometimes.

"We can't both leave the security unmanned, Jason. We would be fired on the spot."

"Right. You know what…you stay here like a sitting duck. I'm bored listening to your mithering already. If anyone pops in, I've gone for a piss." Jason grabs his baseball cap and rolly's and heads on out for a stroll.

"Cameras three and four stay off, ok Steve? D'ya, hear me?" He shouted back as an afterthought. He didn't need him, clicking them back on and beaming his mug all over screen four.

He wandered up to the third floor and reached inside the electrics cupboard on the wall, pressing the lever down, putting the whole of the third-floor corridor into darkness. It was a ritual he liked to repeat, which allowed him to wander along the corridor unseen by any guests. If the cameras were off, then nobody in reception knew it was dark unless a guest complained… by which time, he would switch them back on and dart back to the office.

Hopefully, Steve had done as he was told."

CHAPTER 27

TEDDY

Thursday

"Teddy, can you come up to my office? I need a quick word." Charles' forthright voice booms down the phone into my own, much smaller office.

It's ridiculous. I'm a grown man with a wealth of experience and a ton of satisfied clients, but being asked for 'a word' by the Boss evokes the same queasy dread I experienced as a child when asked to see the deputy head. I'm immediately paranoid, vulnerable and unsure of myself… my conscience shrouded in guilt.

The crazy emails demanding money had intensified the fear by a billion per cent, and the last two weeks have been a blur of frayed nerves and red wine. I feel like shit, I look like shit, and I'm completely in the shit.

I open my desk drawer, grab a couple of Xanax and swallow them back with a mouthful of diesel from my mini-bar, kept in here at all times now.

Charles' office is more like an opulent hotel suite than an office. It spills out over the entire top floor of Delaney & Kilbride, with breathtaking views of St Paul's. It feels more like the set of mad men, such is its grandeur, and it strikes me for the first time that the décor is not dissimilar to The Huxley Hotel. Art décor and old-school glamour fill the room in abundance, and for some reason, the similarity makes me feel even more queasy. Charles has a rather flamboyant gold drinks trolley, heavily stocked in the corner, and I eye it greedily. I feel desperate for another leveller already.

I take in his new, plush and low-seated velvet armchairs, which are flanked by imposing, tall, walnut sideboards. He's a flash bastard; Charles…I think to myself with booze-fuelled irritation. I stick an extra strong mint into my stale, nervous mouth and plonk myself into the spare seat at his desk.

Charles is still on another call, but I have been waved in regardless by his stern secretary, Miriam, and therefore, I'm subjected to an awkward face-off. I'm seated opposite him at his huge desk, and he eyeballs me intently whilst silently nodding into the phone. I wonder, with rising paranoia, if the caller is in fact, my nemesis, Seb.

If Carlsberg made uncomfortable silences (I think to myself), suppressing a sudden, nervous laugh.

"Teddy", Charles booms as his call ends.

"Charles", I reply with an over-the-top smile.

"How are things going at the moment?" He leans back in his chair, head to one side as he searches my soul through the eyes of a human lie detector.

"Fine, yes, absolutely great…why?" I trill, struggling to keep the defensive tone to a bare minimum, but even I can hear my gripped balls beneath the falsetto.

"I know you took up D&K's offer of counselling via the company, and you seemed to pick up for a while… but, I don't know, these past few weeks, you haven't seemed quite yourself, old chap? Clients are beginning to notice Ted. Your biggest clients." Charles looks genuinely concerned about me, and I feel slick with self-loathing.

"You mean Seb Jones?" I just about manage to reign myself in from shouting an Alan Partridge, 'AHHH HAA!!' Instead, I compose myself into a more casual tone of enquiry in the nick of time.

Charles doesn't confirm or deny, but his pursed lips tell me as much.

"I'm sorry, you're right, Charles," I acquiesce. "I've had a few personal issues rear their head again recently and… well, I stopped the counselling… but I'm going to book in with her again this week and get back on track."

"You know I think very highly of you, Teddy… but I am held accountable to the board and alarm bells are ringing louder than Great Paul."

I look vacant, so he bulldozes on.

'The board have suggested your dismissal after the fourth complaint in as many months and from one of our longest-standing clients too."

The blood drains from my face. That filthy rat.

"Don't panic" Charles holds up both hands in a gesture of peace. "You are most certainly not being dismissed, but I am going to have to write you a formal warning to keep the wolves off my own hairy back. You can turn this around, Teddy but do it quickly for your own sake. The board doesn't care for your home life. It's harsh but true. Business is Business, Teddy; you understand that, don't you?"

I head back to my office, swallow another two Xanax and finish off the rest of the vodka. I open my emails, and there, lying in wait, another e-mail from the unknown Hotmail.

From: viewer@hotmail.com

To: tvillandry@delaneyandkilbride.com

Subject: deadline

Time to pass go. Time to collect.

How about you do as your fucking told and transfer the money like a good boy?

I don't want to have to go and ask 'MRS' Villandry. Suzie, isn't it?

Regards,

An old friend

My hand is shaking as I slam the laptop shut. Maybe it is Seb, after all? It must be. I need to get out of here; I can't breathe. It's Thursday, almost the weekend and therefore perfectly reasonable to leave work early. Ten am is pushing it somewhat, but I'm past caring; I need some air, fast.

The walls are closing in, and the acidic taste of sick rises and retreats down the back of my throat. If the stolen money is discovered, then at best, I'm going to prison for a very long time to be ass-raped daily and spoon-fed porridge in the medical room. At worst, this blackmailing cunt may kill my family before my ass even touches Wandsworth. It's too much, my chest is so tight

I can barely breathe, and my ribs and arms ache. I don't have the money. Simple as. I can't pay. I'm fucked.

I order an Uber, and without thinking, I punched in my old address, and I'm heading to Suzie's place. I feel a sudden and desperate urge to see her and the kids. I need some kind of safety net or familiarity to dive into and fast. Suzie's the only person who can anchor me through the storm, calm me down and strop my escalating descent into madness. I want to wake up from this nightmare.

Suzie is surprised but happy to see me, ushering me inside for a cup of tea and a slice of home-made banana cake straight from my old oven. I want to weep against her bosom like a small child at the cosiness of it all. So normal and boring and yet, so safe and perfect. Save me, Suzie, I think silently as I smile at her like a mad man, trying not to cry.

"Are you ok, Teddy? You look a little off-colour. Why aren't you at the office anyway?" Suzie frowns as she lays two plates of the still-warm banana loaf in front of us, next to a steaming, fresh pot of tea, which was part of our wedding dinner service.

"I'm fine, Suz; I just didn't feel too well earlier... maybe I'm coming down with something. I was going to head home to the flat... but then I really wanted to check in on the kids because...." I tail off, as I don't know where I'm going with this half-truth.

Instead, I look anxiously around the kitchen for any sign of that insipid dick, Giles. I can't cope with him today, and my fist twitches with the urge to punch him straight in the mouth.

"Well, I don't want you passing anything nasty onto the kids; thank you, Ted. Lucy has exams next week, and George has a football match at the weekend. It might not have been the best idea to come here if you really are sick." She grimaces as if I have arrived laden with full-on Norovirus and pushes her barstool a little further away from me to a safe space.

"I'm fine," I mutter, taking a large bite of the cake to prove my glowing health. "Where's the lovely Giles anyway?" I enquire, deftly changing the subject.

"Err, he's not here. We've decided to take things a little more slowly. We're on a break." Suzie pours the tea for us both before punching my arm lightly with a half-smile as she clocks my obvious delight.

We chat easily, like we used to, for what must be hours and eventually, she opens a bottle of wine, which I sink into gratefully.

"What about you? I haven't even asked if you're seeing anyone?" Suzie studies my face carefully. It's true; she has never once asked or even enquired as to what I do with my many free weekends and evenings without her and the kids.

"There's been nobody else," I reply, draining my glass. She stares at me silently for the longest time.

I reach for my phone and cancel this evening with Amanda.

CHAPTER 28

AMANDA

Thursday

The mind is a clever and fascinating tool; it often gets stuck in a moment, usually somewhere deep in the past. The brain could quite simply press pause like a TV remote control and stand very still, caught in a certain frame, usually just before or around the time of a shit storm.

My mind felt paused on a time when Ben's best friend still loved me, kept me safe and connected to my brother, regaling me with stories of the brother I could never have known. Through Dominic, I got to know a side of Ben that he had managed to keep well hidden from our family, as all teenagers do.

It turned out Ben wasn't just my kind, annoying older brother. According to Dom, he was funny, really funny. He was daring and fearless. He was clearly more mixed up than we knew, dabbling in marijuana before trying a couple of heavier drugs. He wasn't nearly as well-behaved as my parents or siblings presumed. Turns out, I'm just like him.

It was fascinating for me to hear, and I drank in Dom's stories greedily, always wanting more, relishing in how much closer they brought me to my brother.

Dominic was the only connection I had to the real, true Ben. I don't think he ever realised that when he left for Uni, he took Ben with him.

As soon as I heard Dominic was back, I hunted him mercilessly. Eventually, finding his wife on Facebook. The wife, and the three undeniably, beautiful children, sat beaming from my laptop. It all looked pretty perfect, but I knew it wasn't after catching him with *that* blonde woman. Maybe she was just a distraction, nothing serious, but a clear sign that he wasn't averse to having his head turned. What could be sweeter than finding your first love again?

What I hadn't anticipated was the regularity of his hook ups with the blonde. This was no meaningless fling; it was a full-blown love affair. They stayed at the Huxley every Thursday. The bastard had an actual, proper mistress.

I burned with jealousy and felt the rejection all over again, despite the years that had passed. Dominic had hurt me a billion times, and most friends and family had warned me to stay away from him, but still, I longed to have him back…to have the ending we should have always had.

Up until now, I had kept myself out of sight whilst following him around, quietly seething before I could stand it no longer. I had to make my move.

I felt wild with jealousy. Imagined them swimming together in the clear tank in the centre of their suite, my suite. Tonight, we were all due at the Huxley again, and it was surely only a matter of time before Dom, and I ran into each other one of these weeks. Hopefully, his wife would see me arriving again… if she was still following him. She would have to kick him out sooner or later.

When Teddy cancelled, I was already at the hotel. It was infuriating, but as I had cancelled him the previous week, I wasn't in a position to complain, and he had said he would still pay me. I was about to leave when I happened to glance through to the bar area and couldn't believe my luck. It was rare to catch Dominic alone in either the bar or restaurant as he usually went straight up to his room. Seeing him at the bar, nursing a gin and tonic, was the opportunity I had been waiting for.

"Dom???? Dominic Box?? Oh my God," I feigned surprise with award-winning aplomb.

He leapt off his bar stool and gripped me in a genuine and delighted hug…I vaguely wondered and hoped that Helena was somewhere close by, watching us.

The conversation flowed as he filled me in on his last twenty years, although I barely heard a word that was said, gazing at him with old adoration. Finally, he was here, in front of me, next to me, with me, after all this time. I felt younger and lighter; I felt like me again at last.

'She' had appeared shortly afterwards and clearly despised me at first sight, as I did her. His fancy woman looked even more threatened than I could have hoped. Women are like dogs; we can sniff a love rival out at hundred paces, and this bitch knew what I was after, and I felt her bite.

After she flounced off in a sulk, he stayed for another drink, and it wasn't in my imagination; there was still a connection; I could feel it in the way he stared at me too long, looked at my lips as I spoke…whispered in my ear despite it being quiet enough to hear perfectly well at a distance. He felt it too, I could tell. He had the decency to apologise for 'Kate' and dropped in that it was very casual between the two of them, which spurred me on. I resisted the urge to stick a cocktail stick into each of my eyeballs at the mere mention of her name and instead smiled breezily.

When I could take no more, I made polite noises and called myself a cab. He took my number and hugged me a little longer than necessary.

The anger bubbled inside of me the very second I waved goodbye as I imagined him now heading upstairs to fuck her. I poured myself like molten lava into the back of my Uber.

"KATE", I spat her name out in disgust and pain.

"Sorry love, what did you say?" shouted back the driver.

"NOTHING. I wasn't talking to you." I shot back rudely.

She even looked just like me. What did that mean? That must be a good sign, surely? How could he not want the younger version? The original version? His face had lit up like a candle as he sheepishly explained to me who she was as if I didn't already know.

I jerked my head back in the cab and let out a long howl like an injured animal.

The driver pulled over into the bus lane and spun around;

"Look, are you alright love? Are you hurt?"

"Just drive, please," I sobbed.

CHAPTER 29

KATE

Saturday

'I'm having an affair'... I practice the words over and over in my head, trying desperately to make them more casual... less crushing.

"Tom, we need to talk", I finally say out loud.

The words feel heavy and loaded as they tumble from the back of my throat. Once the button was pressed, there would be no turning back. I'm shaky and faint...about to let all of those clichéd, shitty words tumble out and obliterate the last twenty years of our lives in a couple of small, pathetic sentences.

"I don't have time I'm afraid... I need to head to the office" Tom cuts through my fear and gathers his wallet and laptop, ignoring my ashen face and shaky hands.

"But it's Saturday morning?? What are you talking about?" I'm confused. Have I gone mad? Is it not actually Saturday?

"I know, but we're manic at the office, and I need to finish this presentation. Don't wait up; I'll grab dinner there. Let's catch up tomorrow … a Sunday roast before my flight?"

"Right," I say flatly.

He heads off to Munich on Sunday evening, leaving me to wash away the twenty-five pans he used to cook the three of us a roast. We speak on the phone just the once while he is away and only to discuss a bill payment. By the time I eventually see him on Thursday morning, bounding into the kitchen and beaming like the prodigal husband, I am somewhat despondent. He looks left and right, presumably searching for his welcome banners and trumpet, but I'm preoccupied with escape, desperate to feel like 'me', whoever she is, and desperate to see Dominic. I will save 'The Talk' for another night.

"I thought we could have dinner and watch some Netflix together tonight?" whines Tom sulkily when I remind him that I'm out this evening.

The resentment bubbles warmly under the surface of my skin, but I resist the temptation to ask where the fuck he has been for the last few years when I have fancied Netflix and chill. I take a deep breath and, instead, picture Dominic waiting for me at The Huxley and quickly, my anger dissipates. I no longer have any right to be angry with Tom. It's one all. We are both arseholes. Game set and match.

I make more of an effort to look good tonight as he is taking me to the fine dining part of the hotel to sample the infamous Hux tasting menu. I'm excited in ways I have no right to be and rummage through my wardrobe like a giddy singleton heading out on a blind date. I settle on a black, satin camisole dress …simple but sexy, and I stick some strappy heels into my bag for later. I'm just finishing my make-up when my phone rings. It's Jules.

"Hey, babe", I answer cheerily.

"Hiyyyyyyyyy…" Whenever delivering bad news, Jules has the same prolonged voice of doom as Ross Geller from friends.

"What's up?" I cut to the chase…I haven't got time for chitchat; I'm running late.

"Somebody broke into the office," Dr Death delivers her news brashly, with minimal fanfare.

"Whaaaaat?? When?? What have they taken?" I jump up from the dressing table and pace over to the bedroom window, expecting to see a police car waiting below, with answers and the said robber handcuffed to the back seat.

"They don't seem to have taken anything, Kate… that's the weird thing. That white envelope we had stuffed full of receipts and expenses is the only thing missing, as far as I can see here. It's totally bizarre. The files are all upside down, papers are everywhere, and the office is a complete mess; oh, and our laptops have been hacked but not taken. The police think whoever broke in was looking for something specific?"

"That's so weird," I say, puzzled. We are doing ok, but we are hardly worth breaking into. We have no valuables in the office, aside from the laptops… which they left behind, you say?"

"Yes, both still here. Even weirder, whoever it was, must have had a key. No sign of a break-in or damage to the door or lock. No open windows. They must have opened the main door with a key".

I can picture Jules' face, full of concern…head tilted to one side, lips pursed and a small frown between her threaded brows.

"That's awful," It is awful, but to my shame, I am more concerned with being late for Dominic.

'I can't come over right now... I have plans…I'm about to head out like five minutes ago. Are you ok to handle this tonight? I can speak to the police again in the morning. I will also get onto the insurance company first thing'. I hear the guilty tone in my voice and cringe slightly as I wait for her response.

She's silent for a few seconds, but if she's annoyed at my underwhelming reaction, then she doesn't say so. She must know that 'my plans' involve *him,* and I am effectively putting *him* first, before our business, but she swallows a much-needed lecture and instead agrees to meet me first thing in the morning at the office.

"Be careful," she says gently…hanging up.

I don't have time to fret about this now; I need to order my Uber. Tomorrow morning, I will make a list of old cleaners, temps and interns of old that we have used in the past and then try to work out who could possibly still have a key.

CHAPTER 30

DOMINIC

Thursday

"Are you sure you're feeling ok, Hels? Shouldn't you see a Doctor this week? It's not normal to feel *this* tired all the time, you know. She lays on our huge sofa, tucked as usual under the faux fur blanket and watching TV.

"I'm fine…just a little run down and not sleeping too well at the moment." She answers without taking her eyes off the screen.

"What are you watching?" I try and make conversation, although I have no real interest.

"Big, little lies," she says …finally looking me straight in the eye.

"Right," I say, a little unnerved. "Can I get you anything before I leave? Tea? Glass of wine?

"I'm fine." Her eyes are glued back onto somebody else's messed up life, by the looks of it.

It's Thursday, early evening, and I've popped home from work to see the kids before I head to The Huxley to meet Kate.

"What time is your flight?" she asks suddenly, propping herself up on one elbow and peering at me from over the cushion.

"Err… 9 pm, I think". I'm vague as I stand up and make a show of stretching my old, clicking knees to avoid her gaze.

"Where did you say you were staying ?" She asks

"For fuck's sake…what's with the Spanish Inquisition. My PA booked it…would you like to speak to her? Here let me call her now for you."

She apologises, and I bend to kiss the top of her forehead before heading off upstairs to pack my overnight bag. I feel irritated by her playing the victim… but I carry on regardless.

Tonight, I've booked Kate and I in for the tasting menu. The Hotel is best known for its superior restaurant, 'Hux'. We have eaten in the more casual restaurant on the lower floor dozens of times, but as yet, we haven't gone for the full taster. Word has it; it's amazing, with seven courses and accompanying wines. I've told Kate to wear something sexy, and already, I'm excited by the date-like feel of the evening.

I'm waiting in the bar with a G&T when I spot Mimi at a nearby table, chatting to a fair-haired guy around about my age. God, what was she doing here again? Kate would do her nut, and plus… I had told Mimi that Kate was casual.

Luckily Mimi hasn't seen me, so I ignore her and hope they leave before Kate arrives.

"You look deep in thought?' Kate leans down and kisses me straight on the lips. My slim-fit trousers strain a little at her touch.

"Mmmmm, hello. Wow, you look gorgeous," I say, taking in her slinky camisole dress and strappy heels…. but she isn't listening; she's too busy following my previous gaze.

"Is that who I think it is?" her smile has vanished in an instant.

"Err, yes… Ben's sister," I say in what I hope is a 'don't you dare start" tone.

"Don't you think it's a little weird that, yet again, here she is on the same night as us?" she demands.

"Not really, Kate. She clearly loves this place as much as we do. Are you ok? Are you being difficult again". I pull her hand to sit her down.

"No. Let's go straight into the other restaurant." She stands ramrod straight, towering over me and glaring across at Mimi, who is animated and oblivious.

I drain my gin…a little angry but relieved not to bump into Mimi myself, so this time, I let it go. I lead Kate out of the bar, away from Mimi and down the steps toward the restaurant. Women!

Kate relaxes, and the tasting menu does not disappoint. We feast on cauliflower puree with asparagus, seared Scottish diver scallops, lobster terrine with lemongrass, pork belly braised with apple mousse and the finest fillet mignon. Just when we think we can no longer breathe, we are presented with a tiny but superb, flourless chocolate and almond cake and a selection of French cheeses.

"That was amazing," I say, leaning back in my armchair.

"I can't breathe. I feel so greedy. I shouldn't have eaten so much," Kate says, looking mildly cross with herself as she runs her hand, self-consciously, over her tummy.

"Do you think you've put a little weight on?" I ask her.

"Er…no, I don't think so…I just meant I was full… why… do you think I've put weight on?"

"I still like you even with a bit of extra timber" I give her a wink.

She slams her fork down.

"Omg…are you starting an argument again?" I'm getting a bit pissed off now," I tell her. Fucking hell… She was the one who called herself greedy, not me.

Her phone rings, but she silences it and takes my hands.

"No argument", she smiles.

The restaurant is alive and buzzy tonight, with live music playing from the corner of the room. A young, cool jazz band, wearing flat caps and trainers, put their own raucous twist onto modern house tunes, which has the whole restaurant smiling and upbeat. I forget the shit storm I'm going to have to navigate at home, and I forget that this isn't quite real and just sink into the moment.

'I must get their details…they would be perfect for one of our Pink Pig events,' Kate is glowing as she loses herself in the music.

Later she tells me that someone has broken into her office, which is a pain in the ass, as she puts it, but her business partner seems to be on top of it, and she dismisses it, wanting instead to enjoy the night and worry about that tomorrow.

"Jules is taking care of it; it's fine". She waves her hand, batting away the problem. Our time is precious, and we have bigger things to discuss than a few stolen receipts.

"Shall we head up to the room, or do you want to watch the band for a little longer?" I ask, already standing up and hoping she is as horny as I am.

"Upstairs", she smiles.

I pay the bill, and we head to the lift. I see the back of Mimi, and her friend disappearing into the lift ahead and deliberately hang back a little. I had forgotten about her.

"What are you doing?" Kate quizzes with a smile as I feign interest in one of the paintings in the lobby.

"These are quite something, aren't they," I say.

"Ok, Andy Warhol…it's time to get you up those stairs" She grabs my hand, and we head into the now empty lift.

The doors are just about to close when a bald guy with a very bizarre moustache squeezes in.

"Fourth-floor pal," he says with a wide smile as I hit the lower button for him and raise an eyebrow at Kate. She scrunches up her nose to acknowledge his strangeness, and we stifle a drunken giggle.

JASON

> *"That weird bloke was sniffing around again, Jason noted. Occasionally there would be a random like him in the joint. Somebody who lurked around the hotel, somebody who wanted a good old sniff of the*

place but who didn't fancy paying for the drinks or grub.

There had been a homeless fella once who kept trying to sneak up in the lift on the back of another guest's key card. He had been found, laid out in the corridor with his sleeping bag, a tin of beans, but no tin opener… like a dopey cub scout on a camping trip. Joseph was a soft bastard though. He wouldn't let the tramp stay at the hotel for the night, obviously… but had insisted that the kitchen staff bag him up some decent food before they sent him packing.

This bloke doesn't look homeless. He just looks like trouble. He had sneaked himself up in Dominic Box's lift, although Jason felt pretty sure that he wasn't a friend of his or his fancy piece.

He grabbed his pen and made an informant's description of him.

Five foot ten; stocky, bald, dark moustache… moustache is blue/black in colour, definitely dyed. Black bomber jacket, black jeans and boots. He noted down the intruder's arrival time and added "last seen heading to the fourth floor" at the bottom of the page.

"Right Steve, I might bob down to the kitchen and grab a sarnie; I'm starving. Hold the fort, yeah?"

Jason was bored and couldn't be bothered seeing what the bloke was up to.

Leaving all the cameras switched on for a change, he wandered off to the kitchen via the back stairwell, leaving Steve at the helm."

CHAPTER 31

TEDDY

Thursday

The Hux bar is vibrant and more alive than usual tonight, and I tell Amanda that she was right to permanently change our Wednesday nights to Thursday; the place is busier and much more fun as people begin to enjoy their weekend a little earlier. I had cancelled Amanda both nights last week, Wednesday and Thursday, so I needed to make it up to her tonight. For the first time in weeks, I can almost pretend I'm a normal guy again. No cares, no troubles, enjoying a few drinks with my beautiful girlfriend. She isn't my girlfriend, but she does look beautiful tonight.

We chat effortlessly about her childhood home, which sounds incredible, and she tells me of her siblings and her brother, Ben, and what he was like growing up. She chatters with joy about the things they got up to as children and how wonderfully privileged they were with an abundance of love and freedom, not to mention the great schools they were afforded. She visibly lights up when reminiscing about her big brother, and it's both lovely and sad to see. She talks of the troubles she encountered after he died and the unexpected route her life then took.

It's amazing how grief can lead people down such a dark path, and her vulnerability tugs at my heart. I suddenly feel very protective of her. Her parents sound wonderful, and I wonder what on earth they must make of her life choices. I imagine how I would feel if my daughter, Lucy were to wind up working like this, as an 'escort' or had been mixed up with drugs. I shudder at such a horrific thought and quickly shake it off. I want to stay relaxed and guilt-free, just for tonight, at least.

We are a little drunk as we sway over to the lift to head on up to my room. We don't often hang out in the bar and chat like a regular couple, as that's not the deal, but I think Amanda has enjoyed tonight as much as I have. She doesn't normally drink much at all, but tonight she has sunk more than a sailor on a stag do in Brighton and no clock watching from her either.

She looks lovely in tight black jeans, heels and a silk camisole that shows off her toned, lightly tanned arms.

Her hair is shiny and full, and it bounces around her shoulders as we wobble slightly down the corridor.

I know I'm drinking way too much at the moment, but it's been the only way I could forget the emails and impending doom that had been bearing down on me by the hour. Just for tonight, I'd like to forget everything and bury my head in either the sand or her.

Bizarrely, I haven't had any weird emails this week, which explains my calmer mood. No sinister reminder of the ticking time bomb attached to my back like a terrorist. No demands for cash to be delivered have been made today. I don't know if this minor reprieve offers me comfort or gives more cause for concern. The Hendricks has certainly helped take the edge off it, for tonight at least.

Amanda checks her phone in the lift, and I notice her stiffen a little, and her guard creeps back up; I try unsuccessfully to make her laugh again.

"Bad news?" I ask, pointing to her phone, which she is suddenly glued to.

"Bad news and old news, all very boring…sorry. I'll switch this thing off". Her smile reappears, but as pissed as I am, I don't miss the disingenuous strain around the corners of her mouth.

I'm clearly not the only one with problems, but tonight is not the night for sharing them or being miserable. Plenty of time for that when she leaves.

I'm really starting to like her. Amanda has given me back my missing mojo, and I could be wrong, but I sensed that even Suzie saw something new in me that she liked last week. If the emails really have stopped and all this is finally over, then not only will I not be taking any money from anyone… ever again, but I'll suggest to Suzie that maybe we have an actual date night, away from the kids, away from the old worries, especially now Giles has taken a hike. We could see a play or a show, or maybe a band was more her thing. She loved her music.

For now, I get to spend the whole night with Amanda. No waking up alone. We can order breakfast in bed and continue the 'girlfriend experience' until at least eight am.

Swapping from Wednesdays had meant that we could no longer have the Duke of Shoreditch suite on both nights, but if truth be told, I was relieved as the standard rooms were half the price and there was a swimming pool downstairs, so hopefully Amanda wasn't too disappointed to lose 'The Tank".

"Did you bring a swimming costume?" I ask.

"What???" she laughs, shaking her head. "You are so random?'.

"They have a pool downstairs and a gym. I thought you might be missing the tank…up in the Duke. Thought maybe you might like a swim in the morning…with me." I'm slightly self-conscious as I add the last bit.

"No Teddy, I have no costume. Another time though…?" She adds, seeing my slight embarrassment. She leans over and pinches my cheek affectionately.

I feel a little stupid. I may be older than her, and the one funding this whole operation, but Amanda never fails to let me know that she is running the show. She has a knack of belittling me without ever being directly rude. It's quite a skill set, and I should take note and employ the same tactic at my office. Anyway, the gin is making me maudlin…Mother's ruin. I need to snap out of it. There would be little time for a swim anyway as annoyingly Charles wanted to see me again in his office at nine am. A little unexpected, given that we only just had our recent 'chat'. Presumably, he wanted a follow-up on my 'mental state,' as he liked to call it. I felt like sticking one of those joss sticks up his arse…see how mindful he felt about that, the patronising wanker. One thing's for sure; I would need to inhale a whole bottle of Listerine between now and then with the amount of booze I've knocked back tonight.

CHAPTER 32

AMANDA

Thursday

Knowing I was spending the whole night here at the hotel with Teddy had taken away the usual pressure of constantly monitoring the clock, checking my phone for bookings and generally speeding things along in a bit of a frenzy to maximise my earnings. Tonight was different, I felt completely relaxed for the first time in weeks, and it felt nice.

The bar was buzzing tonight, full of the wild and eclectic. East London's finest. The music was something Latin and moody, and that only added to the sexy ambience of the evening. The rowdy group, who had been sat by the bar earlier, were already up on their feet and attempting some kind of salsa meets dirty dancing moves, roaring with laughter and ordering cocktail after cocktail.

I hadn't been this drunk in years, and it felt great. Screw Jimmy and his disgusting threats.

Tonight, I wanted to have a little fun, and I wanted to feel safe. Teddy was the perfect man for the job. Rather surprising is just how much I'm enjoying his company out in the open…in real life. Much more than anticipated (maybe it's the margaritas. It's been a while), but I haven't spent my time searching for Dominic across the bar or restaurant as now that he has messaged to say he wants to meet me, I can relax a little.

Teddy opened up to me tonight and talked a lot about his family, his ex-wife and their children. He met Suzie at work. She was the junior PA of his CEO when he first joined D&K. It had been a whirlwind, passionate romance with a quick marriage and, surprisingly, lots of travel. For their honeymoon, they had taken a year off work together to travel around Asia, which made me choke a little on my drink. It seemed so carefree, so hedonistic, so very, 'un – Teddy'.

When they returned, Teddy had re-joined D&K with his old boss, Charles. Suzie was pregnant by then and decided to stay home. He clearly still adores his ex-wife, and it's lovely to hear how well he speaks of her, but I feel a little sad for him too. Unrequited love…is there anything more painful. I should know.

At one point, he drags me up and starts to spin me around alongside the drunk salsa group. We sway and twirl and grind hips, giggling before we fall naturally into a kiss. We pull away, surprised with ourselves, and I feel unusually bashful.

"Let's head upstairs," I say, taking his hand and leading him back to our table to collect our things. "I couldn't drink another drop. I'm well and truly done, Teddy Edwards." He slaps me on the arse, and we head out of the bar.

We giggle and stumble into the lift like any other ordinary, tipsy couple.

My phone beeps, and just like that, my buzz is killed as Jimmy's name flashes up to haunt me. Another warning and a final threat over collecting the money.

WhatsApp – Jimmy

"Thinking of coming over to ask Teddy for the cash myself?"

My heart hammers in my chest, but I recover my composure as soon I clock Teddy eyeballing my phone with one raised eyebrow.

"Old news and bad news," I tell him dismissively, closing down any further questioning. I have decided that I can't involve Teddy in this. It's unfair, and he clearly doesn't have as much cash as I thought. I'm going to have to look further afield for someone who can help me pay off this debt. It's the reason I decided to drink tonight, as God only knows what will happen to me when I tell Jimmy that I still don't have the money for him. A twist in my sobriety is the least of my concerns tonight.

Teddy waffles on about swimming. He's such a dork sometimes, as if I'm here for a swim. He's really quite sweet, despite being wet behind the ears for a grown man, but I like him a lot. He's becoming a good friend, and I haven't had a true friend in a long time.

As we sway up to the top floor, I gasp loudly…

"What is it? What's the matter? You look like you've just seen a ghost?" Teddy half laughs but holds my shoulders in concern.

I squeeze my eyes and blink again. God, I'm going mad with all of this stress, or maybe I'm more pissed than I thought. There is nobody there, and the corridor is empty, but I could have sworn I saw Jimmy outside our door. I need to sober up.

"I'm fine. I just need some water. No more cocktails for me, big Ted', I say, giggling with relief.

JASON

The Last Night at The Huxley

> *"Jason eyed the 4th-floor corridor from his screen with a knowing smirk. He knew exactly who was in most*

of these rooms and what many of them were up to. Hell, he could make a fortune blackmailing this shower of shit with his CCTV tapes and little black book of dates and times, and he had seriously considered it. It was a "pension" of sorts to make up for the minimum wage bullshit they palmed him off with here. He felt certain he could wangle a fair amount of cash out of these tossers if he told them what he had on them. 'Hush money'…yep, he would happily stay hush for the right price. He clicked on camera seven for a beak around the place. The random guy with the tache was back in again. Maybe he had the same idea, or maybe he was one of those private investigators booked by somebody's spouse. Jason was excited at that little thought, his imagination going into overdrive. A private investigator paid to catch them doing the nasty. He laughed out loud to himself.

"Naassssttttyyy," he shouted out in a mock American accent.

"What?" said Steve, looking as irritated and confused as always.

"I said they are a nasty bunch this lot, Stevo. Up to all kinds." Jason pointed at the screen with a wink.

"Shouldn't you be monitoring the public areas and not the private bedrooms?"

"Oh, bore off, Steve. Lighten up and give your legs a stretch up the stairwell. Go on…it won't kill you."

He sighed, but to Jason's surprise, Steve stood up, stretched his arms up and then disappeared out of the door."

CHAPTER 33

KATE

The Last Night at The Huxley

Meeting every week no longer felt enough. Now that I had admitted to myself I was in love with Dominic, I ached to meet him all day and all night. The craziness of the situation was spiralling out of control, and it felt like a crash was imminent.

"Tom, have you seen my oyster card?" I yell as I tip the contacts of my handbag onto the floor of the hallway.

"It was in the study last time I saw it," He calls from upstairs.

I'm late as usual and heavy-handedly begin to rummage through Tom's desk and drawers, turning them upside down as I hunt for my pass. I haven't got time for this.

It catches my eye on the other side of the room, just where I left it, on top of my magazine. I curse and hurriedly try and cram all of Tom's papers back into the drawer…that's when I see it. A large white envelope full of receipts. They are my receipts…the stolen business receipts. How bizarre…I'm losing my marbles. I must have brought them home after all.

I've mentioned another Pig event to Tom, and I'll be away in Manchester tonight; I explained as briefly and casually as I could last night… before I went up to bed. Tom had waved a hand in silent acknowledgement whilst carrying on his work in our study until late into the night.

Tonight, at the Huxley, the restaurant is particularly busy for a Thursday night, and it puts both Dom and I on edge. Although the hotel is quite quirky and still fairly unknown, there is always the risk of somebody being here who knows either him or me. He had bumped into his old friend's sister here, for god's sake. Although she posed no threat to us, it proved, we still needed to be more careful and maybe think about looking for a new hotel.

Dom seems distracted tonight; in fact…he's been a little distracted and distant the last few times we've met…I brush away the anxious thought…he's right;

I'm not myself at the moment…it must be the stress of knowing what I have to now do in terms of telling Tom.

"I can't meet next week, unfortunately…I need to go back over to New York for a conference?" He makes it sound casual as he rips apart a piece of walnut bread and smears it with thick butter, not looking at me …and yet, he's never cancelled one in over twelve months.

I gulp my wine and nervously look around the restaurant.

"How long are you there for?" I ask, topping us both up a little.

"JESUS, KATE…What's with the fucking Spanish Inquisition?" he explodes.

I'm so shocked at his reaction; I pour the wine straight onto the white linen.

We are distracted from an argument and turn to see a clearly, very drunk guest swaying from his table and apologizing very loudly to the waitress. I recognize him vaguely; the stocky, blonde guy is another regular at the hotel and always smiling. There aren't too many of us who stay here as often as we do, but I have never seen him quite so hammered.

"Mr. Villandry...allow me?" Joseph clicks his fingers dramatically at the nearest waiter, issuing a silent instruction for the broken glass to be cleared away.

We laugh a little at Joseph's theatrics, forgetting our own crossed words and turn back to finish dinner.

Up in the room, I kick off my long boots and lay clothed on the bed. He does a very quick job of removing my clothes without a single word passing between us.

"God, you are such a great fuck." He shouts suddenly, breaking the sweet silence between us, limbs stretched out and arms above his head. I laugh loudly at his laddish comment, but I'm, of course, delighted with the accolade.

"You're not so bad yourself," I say, mirroring him and laying like a starfish on my back as my breathing regulates.

We lay very still for ages, un-touching. The weight of the world is pressed heavily on my body tonight, and I welcome the space he gives me.

"Are we really doing this?" I ask.

"Doing what?" He jumps up and grabs his phone.

I let the question hang and instead watch his handsome profile as he begins to reply to emails.

My mind drifts to Tom and Freddie and inadvertently to Connie, and without realizing it, the outer corners of my eyes are wet again. Years of silent, warm tears drizzling like rain onto those white sheets. Since I learnt how to cry again, I can't stop. He doesn't notice, and I'm glad they are private tears. I grieve alone, as always.

I need to see Dr. Steinberg. I can't wait another week until the next session. The walls are closing in, and I can feel myself slipping down into a dark hole. I can't afford to free fall completely, I have Freddie to think about, and I steady my breathing and calm my whirling thoughts as I try and think, as always, of still water. Calm, clear water, cooling my thoughts, steadying the storm. My breathing begins to slow.

I curl my body towards Dominic, and we lay a little twisted. I'm conscious that the weight of my big head might give him a dead arm, and I wriggle around, unsettled and a little restless.

The loud ring makes me jump for the second time tonight. Glancing at Dominic apologetically, I slide off the bed and reach down for my bag.

Several missed calls and a WhatsApp ping as I pick up my phone.

21:05

Thursday 12th November

WhatsApp

Jules @ TPP

Kate, call me asap… just had Tom on the phone, and he's not happy! What event? Are you with him? JX

The colour and heat drain from my face as I hand the phone to Dominic.

He reads quickly, hands it back and shrugs nonchalantly.

"Just ignore it."

I can tell he's annoyed; the mood has changed, and he jumps up and moves into the bathroom before I hear the shower turn on.

"Order us some drinks up here", he snaps, sounding a little moody over the avalanche of water.

I quickly hash out a message to Tom, trying to keep the tone breezy and ignore his seventeen missed calls.

"Hey, Jules has completely forgotten about the event; I'm here alone... running around like an idiot...super busy. Call you in the morning. K X

He reads it and calls immediately, but I flick to silent and throw the phone onto the armchair. I hit the hotel phone instead and order a bottle of champagne. I'm feeling more in need of a brandy, to be honest, but I don't want to spoil our ritual and kill the mood more than I already have. It will be fine, I tell myself; stop panicking; I'm being paranoid...Tom is probably just calling because he can't find his charger or headphones or something stupid. I breathe and head to the bathroom.

"Room in there for two?"

He doesn't speak as I join him in the bathroom; he just moves away from the water and manoeuvre's me underneath it. My eyes are forced shut as the hot jet of water pelts heavily down onto my face. I wince slightly with pain and gasp a little for air in between mouthfuls of angry water. I feel two strong hands steady my hips and hold me tight under the water before his tongue begins to lollipop lick ever so gently between my legs. The sensation of the hot water, the pain on my face, the inability to move and the intense tingle from his tongue is spectacular, and I cry out under the noise of the jet. Cupping my breasts tightly, I roll each thumb over my excited nipples and tilt my head further back under the water as he passionately French kisses my hot pussy over and over.

Dropping to the floor of the shower, I grab his face and kiss him again and again, tasting myself in his mouth. Our tongues never leave each other as he picks up each of my legs, wrapping them around his back and sliding me on top of himself before plunging deeper inside than I thought possible.

I cum again, but he hasn't finished with me and lifts me over to the bed. We are still dripping wet from the shower, but he lays me back on the bed, turning himself around and lowering himself over me in a sixty-nine. I take as much of him as I can in my mouth, licking and sucking greedily and running my tongue over his smooth balls as his mouth simultaneously clamps over my pussy. I'm so hungry for this man that I desire so badly that I don't understand. He turns back around and enters me more slowly, this time breathing heavily as we writhe deeply together.

"I love you, Dom," I whisper into his ear. He doesn't reply but kisses me again… hot tears roll slowly down each cheek, and I don't even know why. Tears of guilt, grief…something else I can't quite reach. I let myself go.

"Are you ok?" he eventually asks after we lay in silence for a few minutes. He turns on his side away from me, and I curl into his back.

The knock at the hotel door allows him to escape my clutch, and he jumps up like an excited teenager; "Champagne baby."

I hope you're not going to answer the door like that?" I manage a smile, nodding my head towards his still semi-hard-on. I never tire of looking at his body; it's incredible; there is just no other word for it. Tall, broad, lean and muscular, it's a body owed to a much younger man than he is.

He grabs one of the complimentary white robes & throws the other one across the bed to me. It lands heavily over my face.

"Oi, thanks mate", I giggle, wriggling into it and yanking open the sash window to release the smell of sex over an oblivious East London.

I hear the muffled tones of the bellboy chatting at the door and the clink of glasses as I reach across to my bag and risk another furtive glance at my phone, just in case.

My heart stands still, and the blood drains from my head to my toes in a split second… cold sweat forms across my skin. Eighteen more missed calls from Tom and another WhatsApp message from him.

22.15

Thursday 12th November

Tom: "I know where you are".

JASON

The Last Night at The Huxley

"Jason eyed the image of the bell boy with his silver-plated ice bucket and a bottle of fancy, expensive champagne. He watched with growing irritation as the lad dutifully frog-marched Dominic Box's order up to The Duke suite.

"Flash bastard", he muttered. How great it would be to watch the "real show" inside that room. God only knew what they all did behind those heavy oak doors, but they were certainly getting more action than he had experienced in a long, long time. He swallowed back the mix of hot bile and burped in disgust.

Steve had been gone way longer than his break allowed, and Jason didn't know whether to feel pissed off or impressed with this new, bad Steve. He couldn't find him on any of the cameras, so God only knew where he had wandered off to. Nosey bastard."

CHAPTER 34

DOMINIC

The Last Night at The Huxley

I close the door on the bellboy and my bad mood and perk up at the arrival of the cold champagne and flood of endorphins surging around my groin.

God, I needed this, I needed her, but now I'm starting to wonder…the cost, the hassle, the upset, Mimi turning up…maybe it's just easier for everyone if we stay as we are.

I need to tell her to hold off telling Tom until I can think straight. Fuuuuuuck, I really don't need this right now.

Kate's sad and low tonight; I see it in her face; it's probably a mistake we met tonight as she's not in the mood to enjoy it…it's a waste of both our time.

I'm surprised she still ordered champagne. She's trying hard to keep things light, despite her upset.

I take the champagne bucket over to the table and pour two glasses.

"Shall we watch a movie in bed?" I ask before noticing her grey face, shivering at the foot of the bed.

"He knows", her voice comes out a little strangled. She scrabbles around the room for her clothes while I quickly play catch up with what she's saying.

"I can't find my knickers. Oh God, oh Gooood," she begins to whimper before breaking into a full anguished sob as she grapples angrily with the twisted knickers still trapped in her tights.

"Kate, what's the matter? What do you mean?" I move towards her, but she jerks back as if I have hurt her.

"Don't!!!" she orders. "Tom. He's on his way."

Her face is contorted, and track mark tears roll from her eyes to her chin; her nose drips, and her green eyes look wide with terror. Grabbing her coat and bag, she shakes her head and bolts for the door, leaving me to call out after her, still holding the two flutes.

As the door slams behind her, I spot her phone on the armchair. I grab it and run back to the door.

"Kaaaaaate," I shout into the hall. The lights in the corridor are out, and I can barely see a thing. Fuck, I can't be chasing her like this with my dick hanging out. I go back inside.

The phone vibrates in my hand, she must have switched the ringtone onto silent, but I see Tom's name glaring at me in angry blue lights, goading me to answer. I stare at it silently until his name disappears. A WhatsApp quickly follows, but I can see only the first line and don't know her passcode.

WhatsApp

10.19 pm

Thursday 12th November TOM

"WHICH FUCKING ROOM ARE YOU IN? THEY WON'T…"

My chest tightens. He's here… this is actually it.

I sit on the end of the bed for a second to collect myself…fuuuuuuuck. My throat is burning as my brain processes the enormity of what is about to go down.

I grab her phone and head into the unusually dark corridor, striding blindly and vaguely towards the lift that has brought us up here so many times before.

I need to make sure she doesn't do anything crazy and fess up.

JASON

The Last Night at The Huxley

"Nice of you to join me for the rest of your shift, mate." Jason tutted as soon as he saw Steve sauntering back in.

"You told me to go… and to be honest, Jason, I was tempted not to come back. I'm not sure I can stand much more of your weird ranting." Steve shook his head and sat back in his seat, shoulders hunched and his face drained.

"Well, piss off back to Sainsbury's or wherever it is they hired you from then." Jason spat his words into Steve's tired face and grabbed his baccy tin for his own break.

"Have you nicked my lighter?" he growled at Steve as he swept his hand around the crammed drawer. He felt annoyed having to even address the fucker again after his little outburst.

"I don't smoke," Steve said flatly, eyeing Jason with equal irritation.

Jason held his middle finger up close to Steve's eyeballs before heading back down the stairwell and sticking his head into reception. He could hopefully collar one of the doormen for a lighter instead.

"Sir, if you would like to calm down, please. As I explained, we have no guest under the name of Kate Golding booked here this evening, so if you would kindly…."

Jason watched with a smirk as Joseph, the maître d, flapped around in reception, trying to calm some ranting guy down.

"She is HERE with someone else!!!!" The tall, blonde guy bellowed as the two doormen moved in aggressively to restrain his arms. Both looked drunk on their newfound power.

"It must be under HIS name?" he spat again.

" Pretty, long blonde hair, 5'6, …you must have seen her??? She was wearing a mac, beige… you know. CHECK AGAIN and get your fucking hands off me!!!" he started to kick out like an untrained mare.

Jason darted back into the stairwell. Shit was about to go down, and he wanted a front-row seat."

CHAPTER 35

TEDDY

The Last Night at The Huxley

Talking to Suzie last week had filled me with a new sense of hope that I hadn't felt for a long time. Could it be possible that she still loved me? The blackmailing had stopped, and Amanda and I had managed to let our hair down the last time we were here. Finally, things felt like they were turning a corner.

So, when it all came crashing down, it had felt even more catastrophic.

It had taken only days for my life to descend into complete hell. The blackmail had stopped, but it didn't matter; it was too late. The emails had been intercepted at work, and thanks to our excellent cyber security, my life had imploded.

I feel broken as I wait for Amanda to arrive. I sit still on the hotel room floor, listening to the faint huff of my breath.

I scrunch up the cheap A4 notepaper and begin my third attempt. A suicide note should surely be a little more upbeat. I don't want to be remembered as humourless as well as a liar and embezzler. I can't change the lies; I wish to God I could turn back the clock, but I'm resigned to the fact that it's just too late for that, and besides, everyone will know the truth by now...even Suzie. There's no turning back.

I swallow hard as I sneak a glance at the flashing digits on the radio clock.

Seven forty-five pm and almost nine hours since Charles had stood by and watched me pack up seventeen years of my working life into one tatty, plastic tray. He had been a pretty fair boss despite being pompous.

His all-year-round golf tan had visibly paled as he watched me. His luminous, expensive veneers, hidden behind tight white lips, and even his hard, brill-creamed quiff had collapsed into a flaccid curl. It limped across his shiny forehead in dismay at what a giant, fat letdown I was.

I rub my aching arm and grimace at the humiliating memory of this morning.

I take another gulp of wine and roll my temples to ease the thudding jar behind my right eye, which is twitching uncontrollably all by itself.

I can't shake the awful image of Dougie, head of security, such a gentle giant underneath his menacing security garb. His embarrassment was shiny and pink as he followed orders to manhandle me through the busy, open-mouthed office. The same Dougie who had nodded and peaked his cap at me for at least twelve of my golden years. He had barely looked at me today, visibly upset himself. He shook his head, lowered his eyes to the floor and walked away. His disappointment had burned more ferociously into my conscience than Charles' ever could.

'You know, I have no choice but to contact the police Teddy...you do know that, don't you?'

Charles' New York twang, still heavy after twenty-five years working in the Mayfair office, now wobbled as he shouted the words up toward the heavy ceiling, turning slowly away from my pathetic sight.

Why in God's name had I carried on stealing? I was shaking as I left the building. Why? Why? Why? I was in a lot of debt; it was true… but so were a billion other people, and they didn't resort to fraud. I really hadn't needed the money that badly, not after the kids had finished school. All these years of getting away with it, until now, when these sudden and relentless emails had threatened me daily. My anger soon shifted away from myself and towards the cunt that had brought me down. The email address was an unlisted Gmail, and so far, no amount of digging could trace it back to the perpetrator, but it had to be Seb… or someone connected to him.

Yet, Seb had been the only one to call today to leave a message of support. He had sounded genuinely upset that I had betrayed him but also upset that I had lost my job and that it had come to this. He certainly didn't sound like someone who had been blackmailing me. It didn't add up.

I had tried all manner of defence with the blackmailer these past few weeks. First, I denied all knowledge, and eventually, I admitted the accusations. I had pleaded for his silence, even offered to pay everything back in more slow and manageable amounts. I had bargained with him…offering a percentage of what I took… and finally, I had threatened retaliation.

I entered the building each morning like a dead man walking, waiting for the shoulder tap, and today it had finally come… but not from the blackmailer.

I swallow another couple of meth amphetamines and glug them back with the last of the wine. A quick call to room service to order another bottle, and I pick up the hotel pen once more and begin a new page.

"Dear Susannah,

It may seem terribly cowardly, but I want you to know that this is the only way to rid us of the debt I have created.

I've made some awful decisions, Suzie, but you are the best decision I ever made. You need to trust me on that, at least. They can't come after you and can't touch the house or any of the I.S.A's as long I am gone, and that's why I have to do this.

I'm in a lovely hotel which I know seems frivolous given the circumstances, and bearing in mind, I won't be hanging around for the full English in the morning… but call it one last hurrah, and frankly, I have worked too damn hard over the years to see out my final hours at some shitty little flat. I know you'll understand.

Anyway, I want to apologize profusely to you and the kids (not really kids anymore, but still) for getting this all so very wrong and for this hopeless mess. I hope that someday you will be able to forgive me...maybe not now, but further down the line.

You should know that not one penny of the money I 'borrowed' has been spent on mortgage payments for your home, and for that reason, you can have a clear conscience and will owe the people I stole from nothing. I promise you that.

The reality is I struggled to cover the cost of everything for all of us. Simple as that. I'm a little drunk at the moment; I think I told you that already. I'm feeling very death row about it all, so I'm choosing my last supper. Can you guess? We played this game at so many boring dinner parties over the years. Fillet steak - medium rare, of course. Fries and a side order of creamed spinach. I've had a nice bottle of Barolo, and I might even order a cheeseboard. No need to squeeze myself into slim-fit trousers before Christmas, so why not face-plant the double Gloucester?

You would laugh; I've even bought a packet of Marlboro's. I feel like a student again.

Thank you for the wonderful, wonderful memories, Suzie. Take care of George & Lucy.

I will love you forever Suzie."

T

X

There was no other choice for me now. The job I loved had destroyed my marriage, and now it would destroy my entire life. I faced the prospect of never working again in the industry that I loved so much. I would be struck off for sure; my excellent reputation was ruined in one black, round-robin email.

No wife, no kids, no career, no money or dignity left to carry me through. The stress of it all had made my scalp burn like fire and my heart race night after sleepless night, and I couldn't wait for it all to end. The arse of it all, I knew it was entirely my own fault, and so it seemed only right that I should bow out gracefully.

In Japan, businessmen regularly took their own lives with some element of honour rather than stigma and were applauded for "saving face". For my family, this was the least I could do to spare them any more shame. Now I had decided to end my own life; I felt the happiest I had felt in a long time…I bordered on manic from the joy of having peace in sight. The amphetamines and booze were possibly helping, but really, I had nothing to lose anymore, and the thought made me feel a little crazy.

There was just one thing that I hadn't been able to get out of my mind, and that was which son of a bitch had been blackmailing me. If it hadn't been Seb, then who? I had eyed every colleague with suspicion over the last few weeks, even Dougie on security. In one of my lowest hours, I had even wondered if it might have been Suzie (much to my shame), but then it came. With a sudden bolt of clarity, a lightbulb switched on somewhere in the back of my brain as I called Bissett's agency to cancel *her*. The only person I had ever confided in over this whole sorry mess was… Amanda.

As the realization hit, rage rolled around my belly like food poisoning. I called the agency back and told them I had changed my mind. I would like to see her after all, and yes, for the whole night, please. I washed down the rising lava in my throat with more and more red wine and just waited. She would be here soon.

Her silly coded knock breaks through my dark thoughts.

'Hold on!! Just a minute,' I shout over to the heavy, wooden door as I drag myself off the floor. My leg is cramped from being sat for so long, but I feel lighter than I have in months. A little lightheaded from the wine perhaps and a little buzzy from the amphetamines but lighter all the same… Whooooa

I stumble as I pull back the heavy door,

'Hi Teddy', she breathes...

"Hello Amanda."

JASON

The Last Night at The Huxley

"The lights were bright and intrusive as Jason reached the fourth floor. Squinting with irritation, he reached inside the cupboard that housed the heat and electrics and with a quick yank of the red leaver, he had plunged the corridor into darkness. Nothing but a faint buzz hummed over the hotel corridor.

Jason lingered outside Teddy's door, tonging the inside of his cheek and revelling in the darkness of the corridor. He had always loved the dark, even as a child. When most kids cried for their mums to leave the landing light on, Jason would get out of bed just to switch them off. The dark gave him the freedom to roam unseen, unheard, unnoticed.

The faint hum of the electrics was interrupted suddenly by the ping of the elevator arriving on the fourth floor. Jason kept his back pressed to the wall and watched with curiosity as a stocky dark shadow emerged from the lift. The light from the elevator briefly lit his bald head and twisted moustache. Jason could spot a fellow wrong un' at a hundred paces, and this bloke had trouble written all over him.

He faintly recognized the guy. Yes, it was the strange bloke that had been sniffing around the hotel recently. He wondered if he might well be one of those Private investigators after all and smirked with pleasure…He could taste trouble in the air."

CHAPTER 36

AMANDA

The Last Night at The Huxley

I felt panicked tonight as my Uber turned into Shoreditch High Street, and I spotted the tall windows of The Huxley Hotel coming into view by the East Green.

The text messages from Jimmy had become more erratic over the last couple of days, and nothing I said seemed to appease him. I had taken to sleeping with the bread knife under my pillow now as well as carrying it in my bag, fearing his sudden appearance, ready to teach me a lesson whilst re-arranging my face.

I had never wanted to involve Teddy in any of this, but I had been desperate. Initially, I had thought Teddy was the answer. His rich clients could surely help pay Jimmy off. Ted had already been squeezing them for a little extra cash for years; he had told me so in a late-night confession. What was a little more to him or to them? I had set up a fake Gmail account and false bank account, and after initial reluctance and anger, Teddy had finally replied to the emails, begging for another couple of days and swearing to transfer the money in exchange for silence.

All being well, and if Teddy panicked enough to comply, he had been due to transfer the hundred grand by last Friday. Forty-five for Jimmy and fifty-five for me, just in case Jimmy ever came back for more. Except the fucking idiot hadn't transferred the money.

Inwardly I was fuming with Teddy at first and considered grassing him up to his boss out of pure spite… but then I calmed down as it became very apparent that he didn't have half as much money as I had first presumed.

I stopped the emails to him last week, but I should have known better than to mention Teddy's name or details to Jimmy. I had only thrown him into the fray to bide me some extra time and to let Jimmy know that I did have a cash cow. Jimmy leapt on that lead and had taken to mentioning Teddy's name in every message he sent. It scared the hell out of me. I was scared for myself, but now I was more scared for Teddy.

Jimmy's messages had become sinister in their newfound calmness this week, and I felt permanently clammy with fear.

I had panicked when the agency called tonight to say that Teddy had cancelled me yet again for the third time. I wondered if Jimmy had already gotten to him, so when they called back half an hour later to say he had changed his mind and wanted me for the whole night, I felt pure relief.

I had to be at the hotel tonight of all nights. It was time to come clean to Teddy and tell him what had been going on. I would ask him to forgive me for the stupid emails. I felt confident he would carry on seeing me and maybe even help me…legitimately. No harm had been done, and it clearly hadn't spooked him too much, as he hadn't bothered to pay up.

More importantly, I needed to see Dominic. I had to tell him properly how I felt about him; it was time. For the second time in my life, I needed him to take care of me. The only problem was her, Kate.

I had become just as obsessed with her as I was with him, following her social media posts as avidly as I did his poor wife's. I knew where she worked, and I knew she had a husband and child, possibly two… the posts were not up to date, but I could zoom in on her face, her body, her clothes and her smile as often as I liked. Clearly, she had issues as she was still seeing the counsellor every week too. She wasn't so perfect after all.

I hesitated over sending her husband the letter …I am a girl's girl at heart…but I couldn't let her stand in the way, and she wasn't innocent in all this, so I shouldn't feel too guilty. She was doing a bad thing, and maybe me telling him would help them fix their marriage.

I darted into the foyer of the hotel and pulled out my phone before I reached the lift. I quickly messaged Jimmy to reassure him that he would get his money, but there was a delay. I was sorry for the mix-up and would meet him properly next week to explain. I felt a little calmer at the thought of telling Teddy the truth and being honest with Dom. Finally, this mess might be over.

Teddy opened the door, and immediately I could tell he was pissed and possibly a little high? I noted with amusement.

'Hey babe', he bellows, pupils the size of sherbet saucers.

Teddy is not a 'Babe' kind of guy; he's only ever called me by my full name.

I do a quick three-sixty of the room, my eyes like a Go-pro as I carefully scan, taking in the almost empty bottle of red, lined up next to the finished one, the random screwed-up-balls of paper across the floor, some dubious-looking pills spilt out onto the bedside table....

not blue, so definitely not Viagra I think gratefully. I turn back to Teddy and his black mouth. He looks like a kid with a Vimto moustache as he beams from ear to ear and waves me in. He looks wired, manic even and for the first time ever with Teddy, unease fizzes in the pit of my stomach. Something doesn't feel right.

I accept the large glass of wine from him and take an unusually thirsty gulp before perching on the end of the hotel bed. Teddy remains unusually quiet, and his grinning, wild-eyed stare unnerves me as I wait and watch him.

JASON

The Last Night at The Huxley

> *"Jason was bored of watching the moustache guy like a sitting duck outside Teddy's room. The guy hadn't moved a muscle for at least ten minutes. Jason decided to head back down to the basement before he got his balls busted. As he snaked his way down the backstairs and towards the ground floor, he heard a huge commotion kicking off in reception.*
>
> *Peering around the inter-connecting door between the fire escape and the ground floor reception, he saw the same guy from earlier going berserk at the desk. Jason was almost back down to the basement when he*

realized he had forgotten to switch the goddamn lights back on upstairs. The hotel floors from one to four were still in total darkness. He couldn't be arsed going back up there, but he couldn't afford to get fired either, so he disappeared back into the stairwell."

CHAPTER 37

TEDDY

The Last Night at The Huxley

She sits on the bed, looking sweet and innocent. As innocent as one can look when in fact, you are nothing but a prostitute, a lying slut, cheating, money-grabbing blackmailer and the sole reason my life has turned to utter shit and misery.

Her hair looks shiny and thick, and her face is naturally beautiful despite her over-made-up eyes and glossy mouth. She sits elegantly on the edge of the bed, demurely sipping my wine in her little French coat, like a beautiful spy, which I now know she is.

This is the 'sweet and innocent' woman who has taken away my career, my life savings, my reputation, my dignity and my job; I wince from a sharp stab of anger in my arm again. Now she was going to take a father from his kids...forever.

A cold rage gushes through each vein, fizzing and bubbling under my agitated skin. I try to focus on her beautiful, double-crossing face, but I'm seeing three of the motherfuckers. I sway unsteadily and down the last three-quarters of my glass in one swig.

She is unusually nervous, I can tell. The quiet confidence, bordering on arrogance, that she normally swans in here with has vanished. If I didn't already know what the conniving bitch had just done to me, I might have missed this small nuance, especially as I'm pretty pissed, but the amphetamines have somehow made my mind razor-sharp, despite my wobbly limbs.

'Take your clothes off', I hiss through a wide, fixed smile.

'Teddy, that's very forward for you', she purrs in surprise. Displaying an uneasy smile.

I don't reply, but she obeys for once, sensing the change in my manner and undressing completely before lying down on the bed before us. She begins to speak, to make a nervous joke, but I quieten her.

'Shut up', I whisper as I yank open my belt and pull down my suit trousers, not bothering to take them or my shoes off. This one's for me.

'Teddy, you're hurting me', she yelps, struggling under the dead weight of my highly intoxicated body.

'What are you doing? What's wrong with you tonight, Teddy? Teddy, you're scaring me.'

I grip her arms tightly together above her head with my left hand and slam my right hand heavily over her moving lips, clamping her lying, little mouth shut.

Heaving over her, my heart starts to race far too quickly as the amphetamines rush uncontrollably through my bloodstream, and I feel I'm skipping a beat. The sweat begins to run profusely from every pore, even though I am barely moving on top of her crushed body. I'm feeling strange, and my jaw aches from being set for too long into this wide, gurning mask. I feel faint. I see myself crying as a young boy.... or maybe I'm crying now?

My mind won't steady or focus… but somewhere, I hear my mother saying, 'If the wind changes, your face will stay that way Edward.' She flashes before me, as does a very young Suzie, the kids and my grandfather. All of them jumbled and running across my mind like an old black-and-white film roll on a speedy rewind. I am suddenly aware of the room again as excess saliva begins to drip out of my smile like a dribbling mastiff, landing in big gloops onto Amanda's face.

Her eyes are wide and dilated, but I seem incapable of swallowing it back up. I can't breathe...my grip relaxes and loosens over her mouth. The faint sound of a knock on the door encourages her to scream loudly in my earhole, but she is still unable to move from under my weight. I can hear the sound, but I can't physically move, blink or swallow and my mother is back again, calling me. I see only white.

JASON

The Last Night at The Huxley

> *"Jason was surprised to see the bald moustachioed geezer, still sitting like a guard dog outside Teddy Villandry's room, when he crept back up to the fourth floor. The sudden and loud scream from within the room jolts him a little, but the big dog doesn't even flinch. Jason nods his head with respect. There she goes again, that blood-curdling shriek, but neither men move to help. Both stay perfectly calm and still at their opposite ends of the darkened corridor. The dog guards the door, and Jason guards the dog... with fascination."*

CHAPTER 38

AMANDA

The Last Night at The Huxley

'Take off your clothes', he slurs. I'm not offended by his tone, but I am feeling unnerved as this is not the gentle giant I've been meeting here for months. What is with him tonight? He looks absolutely out of it, and I'm tempted to rearrange the night, only I hate to waste time...and money.

I begin to take off my blazer, wriggling out of my black jeans and crisp white t-shirt, before reluctantly unhooking my lacey bra and panties and folding them neatly on top of my YSL bag (an old boarding school habit). As I lean over my bag, I catch a quick glimpse of my phone, lit with a reply from Jimmy.

WhatsApp Jimmy

"Time's up, collecting in person."

Oh God, he knows this is where I always meet Teddy. I've tried so hard to make Jimmy laugh like we used to in my more recent replies. A new tactic employed in the hope of getting him back on side and engaging him in a little gossip and chit-chat like two old friends. I had even taken to sharing disloyal snippets about Teddy, telling him how strait-laced he was and how boring in bed he could be at times. I wince at the horror of it all. It hadn't appeased him at all. It had backfired spectacularly, and now he was on his way over here.

I had to tell Teddy everything right now to explain what I had been doing with the emails and why. We had to get out of here and head somewhere safe… NOW.

I don't have time to speak, as suddenly and out of nowhere, Ted is on me...his whole weight bearing down as if he's passed out or something. His pelvis crushes me, and I squirm and yelp to try and wake him...but he isn't asleep, and he isn't unconscious.

I quickly realize this is an intentional move by him as he grips tightly at my wrists with that same clown-like grimace he's had since arriving. I'm pissed off now; who the hell does he think he is. I tell him to stop being a prick.

'Shut up', he hisses at me as he enters me unexpectedly and uninvited. He's hurting me, but it's not the sex that hurts, as he's not quite up to it. It's my wrists that burn as his body lands like lead, crushing onto my organs. I hear myself scream, and then quick as a flash, he clamps his heavy hand over my mouth.

Oh God, I feel like I'm going to pass out; I can't breathe; I'm so squashed and gasp desperately for air through my nostrils. I bite as hard as I can on the inside of his palm, and it lifts very slightly, affording me another scream and gulp of air before it clamps down hard again over my mouth and across the edge of my nose.

My eyes are bulbous, bursting out of their sockets as they lock onto his foaming mouth. There is a loud knocking at the door, and I scream again. Like a rabid dog, Teddy's wide, grinning mouth releases huge globs of saliva, which fall heavily onto my face and his own hand before he completely falls onto me, his big head smashing down onto mine.

JASON

The Last Night at The Huxley

> *"The black silence filled the corridor. Jason reached into his pocket and checked his phone. No messages. No one had clocked that he was well over his fifteen-minute*

break time, he realized smugly. He put it back in his pocket and, looking back towards Teddy's room, he blinked furiously, wiping his eyes roughly on his sleeve and squinting. He blinked again as he realized that the shadow of the moustache guy had gone. Jason decided to head back down to security via the stairwell."

CHAPTER 39

KATE

The Last Night at The Huxley

I run blindly, tears and snot merging into one trickle as I choke back the strangled cry in my throat. I hadn't even noticed the corridor was pitch black as I ran from Dominic and our room. It was only on hitting a surprise swing door that I found myself in some kind of stairwell or fire escape. Looking back through the door and out onto the corridor, I see there is nothing but a black hole. Where the hell was the lift? Why were the lights out? I'm shivering, cold and jittery from the adrenaline and taking a deep breath, I decide on the stairwell option instead of the black hole. I tentatively let the drop and twist of the cold, concrete steps guide me down to reception and back to my waiting husband.

It was like a night terror, an out-of-body experience; this couldn't be happening. How could I even begin to explain this to Tom when it didn't even make sense to me? What did he know? How did he know? What would I say? Would I start from the beginning? Should I fess up to the whole horror or spare him some pain and keep on lying?

If I told him I was leaving, would he try and take Freddy…I wailed out with pain at the thought of it all as I put my flat hands against the wall and felt my way further and further down the dark steps.

My mind was racing, even though I had played out this scenario in my mind thousands of times before. I had lain awake on many nights, heart racing and skin burning with cold sweat as I imagined my two lives finally colliding. The hurt and humiliation for Tom, the pain and disappointment for little Freddie, the disgust and anger of our families and friends, the public flogging from acquaintances, neighbours, and school parents who would never understand. It should have been more than enough to make me end this madness months ago, but I couldn't, and I hadn't.

Now it was too late; my thoughts were all over the place. I didn't even know what I wanted. I couldn't live without either of them. My head was spinning; I felt faint.

The beep of a text message interrupts my racing thoughts, and not trusting my balance on the unlit steps, I carefully sit back onto one of them and begin to rummage in my bag for my phone. It was probably Tom again or maybe Dominic, panicking. As my hand roams unsuccessfully around my almost empty bag, a cold realisation washes over my scalp and down to my neck…I don't have my phone…it must be back in the room. If it wasn't my phone…then someone else was clearly here with me.

JASON

The Last Night at The Huxley

> *"Jason knew the stairwell like the back of his hand, and he didn't need any electric light to guide him around the secret pockets of this hotel. He couldn't see her in the dark, but he knew she was there from the smell of her musky perfume, or did she just stink of sex as she felt her way down the steps towards him on the floor below? She was wailing like a strangled fucking cat; it was irritating, and she was sniffing loudly like some snotty-nosed little kid. He waited quietly and patiently for her at the bottom. Jason's phone beeped loudly, alerting her of his presence, and he cursed inwardly, hurriedly switching it off."*

CHAPTER 40

DOMINIC

The Last Night at The Huxley

I reach the lift quickly, knowing the familiar hotel corridor all too well, despite tonight's weird power cut. I had always had a good sense of direction, even as a young boy. At ten years old, "man of the house" after Dad left, I had been left to steer the ship and take care of mum and my sister, but now I hadn't got a clue what direction my life was heading in, I just knew it wasn't a good one. I press ground level, take a deep breath as the door pings and prepare to face Tom and Kate.

I recognise him as soon as I step out.

I wonder if he'll recognise me, after our meeting all those months ago…but why would he? He doesn't even look up, and I stand back and watch him for a minute. He's sat on one of the high- backed velvet chairs that are dotted around a low, heavy oak table full of pretentious magazines. He leans forward, one elbow on each wide-set thigh with his big hands clasped tightly around the back of his neck…he looks braced for a crash landing on a doomed flight which I suppose is not so far from the truth. Two burly security blokes stand nearby as Joseph whispers to another colleague, sneaking nervous glances over at Tom.

Where is Kate? She left a good ten minutes ahead of me…plenty of time to be down here now with Tom but not enough time to have already had it out with him and left. Her absence stumps me as I had expected to face them both together and for him to instantly realise it was me, if only from her reaction. Standing here now, he barely gives me a second glance, and I would be lying if I said I wasn't tempted to just walk on past him and get the hell out of this hotel.

I loiter near the oak table, pretending to pick up a magazine as he reaches for his phone and angrily punches his middle finger over the screen face. Suddenly, my trouser pocket starts to ring loudly. Her phone! It's in my pocket! I gingerly take it out, knowing the answer already and just as I see the name Tom on the screen, his full right hook takes me clean out.

JASON

The Last Night at The Huxley

"Jason wandered back through the stairwell to the connecting door that looked out over the reception. Downstairs, staff could be sacked for showing their mug in public, but occasionally he couldn't resist a peek out into the foyer.

The bitch fight between the two blokes was unexpected, and he smirked in delight as he saw Dominic Box fall down like a sack of shit.

Carl and Danny leapt onto the tall, blonde man to hold him back. He watched the man effing and blinding and shouting his mouth off like some dirty street fighter. Jason kept out of sight behind the swing door. To be honest, he was still shaken up a little after the incident on the stairs with that stupid slut. He wiped the streak of blood from his right hand down the side of his dark trousers. It was time to get his ass back to his desk, pronto."

CHAPTER 41

TEDDY

The Last Night at The Huxley

I splutter and choke back into consciousness like someone emptying their waterlogged lungs after a sea rescue. The sour stench of vomit immediately floods my nostrils as my hand locates the source and unintentionally lands on the wet bile and booze congealing on the pillow beside me.

I feel strange and very, very cold.

I manage to rotate my body, a hulking, ungainly pig on a hog roast, moist and glistening with sweat as I roll over. I feel absolutely huge, like I've doubled in weight and size, as I hoist myself up onto the other side of the king-sized bed, where the pillows look dry. My heavy eyes take in the room, empty but for several strewn wine bottles and masses of scrunched-up paper. What the fuck?

My lids close, weighed down by an unknown fog, and I feel as if I am floating away again.

"GET UP", a deep voice commands in my ear as my eyes flicker back on the room and register that I am, in fact, not alone at all.

Amanda has gone, and instead, I see a strange moustache and the hazy outline of a large male frame. I must be hallucinating as this strange figure snarls in my face, leering terrifyingly over my bed just inches away from my face.

I try and ask, "Who the hell are YOU?" but my mouth just won't work & my jaw feels slack as the left side droops disobediently. Instead, I hear a slurred version of my words reverberating around my lips and the room.

"SIT THE FUCK UP", he growls.

I hoist a little higher and again begin to reply, but my mouth refuses to play ball with my thoughts.

"I WANT MY FUCKING MONEY; YOU DROOPY-EYED CUNT"

I wiggle my eyelid self-consciously, but the left side is just too heavy to open. Is someone sat on my face, I wonder? The innuendo makes me chortle inappropriately, nervous laughter, or am I still high? It really does feel as though a heavy hand is pressed down on my left side, dragging my face south. I try to explain this politely out loud to him, but I am slurring again. Perhaps I'm still pissed?

"WHAT IS WRONG WITH YOU? ARE YOU FINDING THIS AMUSING, YOU FREAK? This is what's going to happen, big boy. You're going to get on the blower and transfer the cash like you were supposed to, and in return, how about I don't slice off your flaccid cock and fuck your own pathetic ass with it…you get me?"

The foamy spit starts to bubble and ejaculate out of my slack jaw like an over-poured cappuccino, causing me to cough and splutter once more. It takes all of my might to try and sit up and comply with this psychotic intruder, but I can feel my body and mind zoning in and out of consciousness.

"Oh, Jesus Christ", I faintly hear him muttering as my eyes flutter.

"That's all I need, *you* carking it… Wake up, you bastard? I can't believe I'm doing this. "Hello, yeah, we're going to need some medical help…my err …my partner has had some kind of stroke or something, I think."

My lids close, and not just the heavy one.

"Mr. Villandry? Mr.Villandry? Teddy? Can you hear me, sweetheart? The soft, gentle voice envelopes me like soft cotton candy as my eyes start to flicker.

"We are going to have to get you over to St Leonard's hospital, my love. You are ok, but we need to run some tests now, okey-dokey?"

The voice is very slow, as if the owner is speaking to a deaf pensioner with Alzheimer's. My eyes flicker open and settle on the green paramedic boiler suit before me. There are two of them, two green suits and that strange man again, the funny moustache. I think I'm going to…

"Paul. Pass me the petri; he's going to vomit again," the slow speaker in the green suit calmly instructs suit number two as I heave and retch over her.

She looks over at the guy with the moustache, "Would you like to come with your partner in the ambulance, or are you able to follow us down in your own vehicle Mr…

PARTNER??????? I think woozily before retching again.

"It's Samuels, err Mr Samuels… yeah, I'll take the Ambo with him," the moustache guy nods over to me.

"Okey-dokey, well Teddy, let's get you onto this stretcher now my love and get you nice and comfortable, ok? Paul, after three. One, two, three, lift."

I am dropped onto the stretcher like a slab of concrete as the green suits lift and drop me in unison and begin backing up towards the door.

"Could you open the door for us, my love? Then we can take the lift down together to the Ambulance."

Another deep new voice interrupts the Green Suit, but I can't raise my heavy head off the stretcher to see whom it belongs to.

"I appreciate that, officer", Green suit speaks slowly to the Police Officer, who is presumably also deaf with advanced dementia. "But as you can see, Mr Villandry needs to get to a hospital immediately. Suspected stroke by the looks of things."

"Amaaada???????" I slur as I try desperately to raise myself up.

"What did he say?" asks the deep voice of the Officer.

"Shhhhh now Teddy, just rest ", comes a soft male voice as a hand strokes my hair. My eyes bulge, and my legs start to kick as I see that it is the moustached thug above me, with one finger pointing up over his curling top lip as his other hand strokes my hair.

"Amaaada??" I warble again as my body jolts against the restraints of the waddled blanket. My voice won't work, but my insides scream, "AMANDA????"

JASON

The Last Night at The Huxley

> *"Back in my seat, I zoom in on camera one and spot the paramedics arriving in the foyer. Christ, that bloke must have really hurt Dominic Box when he took him*

out. What a pussy, causing a fuss so he can put in a fake whiplash claim later. "Where there's blame, there's a claim," I mimic out loud as Steve raises a bored eyebrow.

The medics ignore the scuffling men and hurry straight past them towards the lift. I watch the screen as they go up, two, three, four…ping. Their grainy figures heading clearly towards

Teddy's room.

A commotion on camera one brings my eyes back to the foyer as I spot two police officers arriving and quickly detaining the angry bloke in reception, along with the great Dominic Box. Joseph looks beyond flustered as he flits between the retreating paramedics and the officers. I grab my notebook and notice something red smeared on the back of my hand as I reach for my pen. I wipe it on my trousers with irritation. More of her dirty blood."

CHAPTER 42

DOMINIC

The Last Night at The Huxley

I sit at the empty, long, wooden table in the staff kitchen of the Huxley hotel, holding a tea towel of crushed ice against my throbbing cheekbone.

The kitchen is the antithesis of the hotel. No art deco, no old school glamour; instead, a cosy space reminiscent of old servants' quarters. Simple, rustic, messy and warm, the kitchen is suspiciously empty, except for the uniformed policeman and me.

The other Police officer had insisted I wait here until he had finished speaking to Tom, but I've been here for hours.

My thigh is twitching, and my heart feels like it's about to jump through my chest. Something is seriously wrong here, and I feel frightened. This can't just be about the fight between Tom and me. There are at least a dozen more police officers swarming through the lobby and two guys in plain clothes who, I'm guessing, are detectives. It's chaos; like something you see on the TV, it's?? Fuck, I don't know what this is.

Where are you, Kate? Where are you? I dropped her phone on the marble floor of the lobby when her husband smashed his fist into my face. He must have picked it up, or somebody did. I have no idea where my phone is, either. In our hotel room, I guess.

Where the hell is she? I still haven't seen her. I don't understand. I need to speak to someone.

My mind races at a hundred mph. So, this is it, he knows. Tom knows. This changes everything. I'm going to have to tell Helena everything If Tom isn't already on his way over to my house to tell her himself.

The adrenaline and pain pulsating from my face have given me a cracking headache, and I feel like I could throw up. Suddenly none of this seems very sexy or exciting. I could really do without this fucking drama.

I rerun the events of the night over again in my mind. How had he found out? I need to see her and get the story straight.

I wonder how Tom will react. Surely, he would ask her to leave their home? Maybe not? Maybe he would beg her to stay, to try again. Maybe he could forgive her? I hadn't had the chance to tell her not to leave him.

Arghhhh, I can't think straight. I need to see her and speak to her properly before I speak with Helena. God only knows how I'm going to explain any of this to her. My head is spinning. This is the worst possible way that it could have come out. No way would be a good way, but this…this is beyond. I need to get my story straight and fast.

CHAPTER 43

TEDDY

I'm alive. I'm alive, and I'm surprised that this does not disappoint me. My head feels as though it's been run over by a truck, but I'm still here, and Suzie is here, standing by my hospital bedside.

"Ssshhh, rest now; you can talk tomorrow," she soothes, stroking my hair back from my face as my Mother did as a boy. A tear escapes from my left eye at the loving gesture, and I close both eyes to stop her from seeing any more. The events of the night pound like fists against my brain. I have no idea what Suzie knows about the hotel, the goodbye note I left for her, being fired from D&K, the fraud investigation, Amanda, any of it? All of it? I just know that she's here, and for now, that's all I need.

I need to ask the nurse where Amanda is, but my brain is hurting, and my mouth is clamped tight with a dryness that renders me mute. I think I may have hurt her. The thought brings more tears. I didn't want to hurt her; it just got completely out of control. I must have been out of it, as chunks of the evening remain hazy. God, I'm tired, so tired, but the pounding in my brain keeps me alert and starves me of sleep.

"Mrs. Villandry. We need to ask your husband a few questions if that's ok with you?" A man's firm voice filters into the room, and I open my eyes to see two police officers standing beside Suzie.

"I'm not sure he's up to it yet. You do know he's had a mild stroke? It's a wonder he's still alive…I'm sure you can wait until the morning, Officer?" Suzie takes charge as she always has done. My Suzie.

"We are aware of that, Mrs Villandry, and I can assure you that we won't be causing any further distress, but with respect, it is incredibly important that we speak to your husband about a separate incident that occurred at the Hotel this evening" The officer is polite but assertive, and eventually Suzie gives in and begrudgingly agrees to go and grab a cup of tea.

"Mr Villandry, we just need to ask you a few questions concerning who you were with this evening at the Huxley hotel?"

"Will you need to tell my wife? I ask meekly. "I mean, she's my ex-wife, but I would still like this to be private if that's possible?"

"That's absolutely fine. Your wife is currently unaware of the details. Can you confirm the name of the lady you were with at the hotel this evening, Mr Villandry? One presumes that it was not the (ex) Mrs Villandry?"

"Amanda Moretti," I say hurriedly, ignoring his sarcasm and wanting to get this over with before Suzie returns with her stewed tea and a stewed face.

"You may as well know that she's an escort girl, and I book her regularly through Bissett's Beauty and Massage". I have the good grace to look as awkward as I feel. "Is she ok? Did she say anything about me?" I look furtively towards the door, expecting Suzie to burst through at any moment, ready to rig me up to a lie detector kit. My palms are sweating.

"We haven't managed to locate the whereabouts of Miss Moretti at this moment in time. The CCTV has shown her leaving your room at nine twenty- six pm and running along the corridor towards a stairwell, positioned at the end… which is used as a fire escape. Unfortunately, there was an issue with the hotel lighting this evening, and the image we have is rather blurred. We have no pictures of her leaving the hotel, although the hotel has now been evacuated, and she is most certainly not inside. Did she mention where she might be headed … after your tryst, Mr Villandry?"

"I don't recall her leaving, I'm afraid. I don't know what happened; I must have passed out. I had taken some pills and… the guy, the moustache."

"There was a man with you when the ambulance arrived. He planned to accompany you to the hospital, but he disappeared, according to one of the paramedics who treated you. Do you recall Mr. Villandry? Was this gentleman a friend or fellow guest at the hotel?"

"I think that's enough, officer…you can see this is causing a little distress to my patient" The Doctor's authoritative voice cuts through the room and puts paid to my confessing any further this evening.

"Thank you, Mr Villandry; if you think of anything else, please contact us at any point this evening. Otherwise, we'll be back in the morning when you've had a little rest" the officer tosses a card onto the bedside table, and they nod politely at the Doctor on their way out.

"Jimmy," I say to the closing door.

CHAPTER 44

KATE

I didn't hang around to find out who was in the stairwell.

My heart felt like it might beat right-out of my chest, and fear and anxiety tingled through every vein.

I made my way back to our room... the door was ajar, but no sign of Dominic.

Sitting on the bed, I put my head low between my knees and inhaled deep breaths. I needed to calm down before I threw up or passed out, possibly both.

I tried to think of Dr Steinberg, tried to think of her calm words.

"You are floating in water Kate... nice and relaxed. The sun shines softly onto your face, and you are floating... just floating... as light as a feather. Let your worries or cares float away from you and focus on nothing, other than the gentle sound of the water."

On instinct, I turned on all the taps and began topping up The Tank with more hot water.

I hunted-around the room for my phone, but it was nowhere to be seen... gone. Dominic must have taken it and gone off looking for me.

God... I couldn't think straight.

Tom had no idea who Dominic was or what he looked like... surely not... although he was here and knew I was with (someone), and that was terrifying enough in itself.

I couldn't go down and see Tom now... not with both Dominic and Tom in the lobby together.

I needed to calm down... decide whether it was time for the truth or better for everyone to deny ever being here when I returned home in the morning.

My stomach churned, but I undressed and climbed into the water.

CHAPTER 45

AMANDA

I shiver under the tree, hugging my jacket a little closer for warmth. The East Green is wonderfully busy in the daytime, full of mums and toddlers playing on the little set of swings, which sits in the centre of the heath, along with small groups of office workers eating lunch, chatting on mobiles and smoking a quick cigarette before they returned to the office. The Green is surrounded by tall, black, gothic-looking railings which look scruffy and old-fashioned by day but wonderfully majestic by night, enhanced by the imposing street lanterns that overlook it.

The East Green is adjacent to The Huxley Hotel, and in the dark of night, it is mostly empty aside from a few stragglers from local bars, a couple of regular homeless people, teenage lovers and now, me… a woman apparently on the run. From here, I can hear the sirens screeching to and from the hotel as I sit and wait in the dark.

The sound of drunken laughter echoes through the trees as people cut through on their way to and from the bars of East London. I'm hidden from sight, yet close enough to hear their chatter and listen to their excited wondering as they speculate over the commotion coming from The Hotel.

After fleeing Teddy's room, I had made my way down to The Duke of Shoreditch Suite on the third floor, desperately trying to find Dominic. Hurtling blindly along the dark corridor towards the large door of the suite, I had frozen immediately. The sound of raised voices and crying from behind the door had rooted me to the spot for a few seconds before I darted into the shadows and crouched quietly in the dark, trying to figure out my next move.

Taking out my phone, I decided I would have to call the police. I had no choice. Jimmy was here, possibly sawing off Teddy's ear, this very minute. Kate's husband was on his way over here, possibly here already, thanks to me.

I gave the address of the hotel and our room number to the operator, reporting a violent attack. I hung up just as they asked for my name. They would no doubt trace the call to my mobile phone, but I would have to think about that later.

A sudden slamming door had alerted me to somebody leaving the Duke Suite, and I ran back out into the dark corridor and gasped…Helena Box.

Even in the dark, I could see her face visibly pale when she saw me standing before her.

"You", she whispered, barely audible. "But?" She pointed back towards the suite and then back at me in horror?" I can still hear the curious whimper she had let out; it had sent chills along the base of my spine before she disappeared towards the lift.

I ran towards the suite door and hammered my fists against the heavy wood.

"Dominic, LET ME IN. Dominic," I screamed, banging over and over. Nobody spoke, and nobody came. A sudden whirring sound had interrupted me as I saw a light crawling slowly up each floor of the hotel towards me. The elevator.

I had to get out of here. I had darted into a stairwell and began to feel my way down the stone steps.

I fumble now for one of my thin cigarettes from my blood-stained bag…shaking as I try to rummage for my lighter. They seem suddenly decadent and wholly inappropriate under the circumstances, but I need one more than ever to calm my nerves. I can't find my zip lighter, and more alarmingly … the blunt old kitchen knife isn't in here either. I empty the contents out onto the grass, flustered and panicked. It must have tumbled out of my bag in the stairwell when I fell.

The screen on my phone is cracked in hundreds of tiny places, but it is still alight with the fourteen missed calls and twenty or more short messages. I feel acid rise from the depths of my throat and swallow it down, tilting my head back against the girth of the tree and holding the unlit cigarette between my lips.

I wonder if Teddy is ok. Has he been hurled like a rag doll through the fourth- floor window by now?

I'm sick with self- loathing. I should never have mixed Teddy up in any of this. It's not a world he knows. He doesn't deserve this. He has a family. I could weep for him, but I'm in too much shock to have any other emotion.

My head is throbbing from the gash above my left eye, and I press the back of my hand against it to try and stem the blood. The panic, along with the complete darkness of the stairwell, had made a fall inevitable really, and my head had hit the corner of the bottom step quite badly.

When I felt Jimmy's hands pulling me off the steps, I had fought him like a wildcat in that stairwell, with every breath in my body…except it hadn't been Jimmy.

"Get off me, you mad bitch," The scruffy guy had shouted, as I clawed at his face and bucked my torso back and forward, like a wounded animal. I stopped still. That wasn't Jimmy's voice. For the first time, I looked at him properly and saw the grubby blue security shirt and the pointy yellowed teeth. My blood was smeared on his shirt, and he looked furious.

"I need to get out of here," I screamed at him.

"Off you go, you fucking whore", he muttered as he pushed at the fire escape door leading out towards the Green. He punched the back of my head as I left.

"That's for scratching my face, you psycho." He yelled …but I was gone. Running and running across the east green.

My phone beeps again.

"Where are you?"

I switch it off and wait.

CHAPTER 46

DOMINIC

"Dominic Box?" "I'm Detective Carlisle…the investigating officer. 'Stay seated," he says, waving away my outstretched hand as I sit back on the chair.

He looks rough around the edges, like a boxer, which is at odds with his well -spoken voice. His jaw is square, and his nose looks like it's been broken more than once. His dark slanted eyes stare straight through me, and unusually I feel unnerved by this younger man with his unblinking eyes. Three days' worth of stubble growth and a creased-up shirt makes me wonder if he has even been home for the last few days.

"Look, I don't know what else has been going on here tonight, but my domestic quarrel is not exactly police worthy; I don't want to waste your time. I won't be pressing charges… I deserved it," I say, pointing to my swollen eyelid.

"HE… won't be pressing any charges," Carlisle smirks, turning to the younger, even cockier-faced Detective behind him and thumbing over his shoulder at me. They both share a laugh, and Carlisle shakes his head.

"That's mighty decent of you, Mr Box, but I think we'll be deciding on any charges made here tonight."

"Mac, get Mr Box down to the station for questioning while I go and check where we're up to with the medics.

The younger guy steps forward.

"Detective Macklin," he says coldly. I offer my hand, but he ignores it, clearly taking his cue from the Boss.

"I'm going to need you to accompany me down to Liverpool Street station," he says without explanation, holding his arm out as my prompt to follow.

There are police sirens, two ambulance and a swarm of activity going on as I approach the foyer, making my way out onto the street directly in front of the hotel. I see no sign of Kate or Tom, and I know this fuss can't all be for my scuffle with Tom Golding. This is for someone else.

The interview room at Liverpool Street is cold and grey from wall to ceiling. I ask if I should contact a lawyer, but I'm told it's just a formality, and there is no real reason to contact a lawyer at this stage.

“So, what brought you to The Huxley Hotel this evening?”

Macklin is handsome, also in a rough sort of way, but a little more groomed and ironed than his Boss. He’s also young enough to be my son; I think to myself as he eyeballs me with his bolshie, millennial smirk.

“I was staying there for the night with a friend”, I confirm wearily. I feel drained, and everything throbs.

“What kind of friend would that be then, Mr Box?

He’s getting on my nerves, repeating my name every five seconds, but I swallow my irritation as I’ve had enough trouble for one night, and I just want to see Kate and check she’s ok.

“My friend,” I say self- consciously. It sounds strange, even to me, when spoken out loud.

“Your friend, you say?” he repeats my words slowly, eyeballing me as he scribbles on his pad without looking away from me. He looks smug and amused.

“Look, I think we can cut the crap here’ I snap. ‘We’re having an affair. Yes, her husband caught us at it… and yes, he smacked me in the face. I point to my eyeball for the second time. “As I said, I won’t be pressing charges, so I think we’re pretty done here. It looks like you have more serious matters going on at the hotel tonight, so if you wouldn’t mind, I would like to get out of here and find Kate.

"Mr Box. Your girlfriend is currently having a pool full of water pumped out of her lungs over at the ICU in St Leonards, having been near drowned in your expensive Suite… so let's indeed cut the crap. You can start by telling me exactly what happened when Kate's husband found the two of you "at it," as you say."

"What? Sorry, what are you talking about? She can't? I was with her? She only just left." I shake my head; I don't understand.

"Her Husband has identified her, Mr Box. She's breathing again, just about, but it doesn't look good. So, are you confirming that you were the last person with Mrs Golding this evening?"

My right knee starts to shake involuntarily before I notice my hands doing the same. I'm cold, freezing, and my chest feels tight, wheezy even. I can't take in what they are saying. I feel like I have water in my ears. Detective Macklin is saying something and shaking me. I push at him, struggling to get him off; I can't breathe; he's grabbing at me…

"Mr Box, put your head between your legs and breathe in."

"He's having a panic attack. Go and get him some tea, Gav? Plenty of sugar; we don't need the main witness having an epi. GO," I hear him say to the uniformed officer in the corner.

I sip the tea slowly and eventually start to breathe a little slower. I'm still shaking. I can't take this in; I was just with her; it's impossible to take this in. I insist on calling my lawyer mate at this point, but I don't contact Helena. What can I possibly say to her? It dawns on me that I'm supposed to be in Madrid at a work conference, not even in the country. It's so messed up; I don't know where to start.

Will Bamber arrives within thirty- five minutes of my call.

He looks as always as if he's just returned from a catalogue shoot, tanned, relaxed, and expensive, and I note the young Detective flash a fleeting look of envy at his impressive stature. Will greets me with a half hug and a heavy back pat before he opens his briefcase and introduces himself to Detective Macklin and the uniformed officer. We resume questioning.

"I believe Mrs Golding is in a critical position, Mr Box, so if I may, I will need to ask you a few questions as to your movements over the course of this evening?"

"For the benefit of the recording, Mr Box, can you confirm your full name, date of birth and place of residence."

"Dominic Paul Box, seventeenth of the fifth, nineteen eighty. My address is The Old Vicarage, Marsh Lane, Clapham. I hold my head in my hands as I speak.

"Thank you, Mr Box. Now, can you tell me the nature of your relationship with Mrs Katherine Golding?"

"I have known Mrs.… Kate…I have known Kate for around twelve months. We are close friends; I wouldn't hurt her; I did NOT hurt her."

"When you say friends, Mr Box, could you be a little more specific? Where you and Mrs Golding lovers?"

My head hangs low with fury at being caught out.

"Yes."

"Have you been lovers for the full twelve months of knowing one another?"

"Pretty much" I rub the rough stubble across my chin awkwardly and take a quick glance at Will. Will knows Helena incredibly well, but if he feels any surprise at this revelation, he has the good grace not to show it. I wonder if he is remembering our chat at The Iris café.

"Again, I'm going to have to ask you to be more specific, sir. Can you clarify what you mean by 'pretty much?"

"A week after we first met. We slept together a week after we first met, so yes…pretty much the entire twelve months."

"Can you tell us how you first met Mrs Golding?"

"We saw the same therapist…you know, counsellor," I say.

"And that would be a Dr.…" The sergeant shuffles through a couple of papers, pulling one out to the top and squinting. "That would be a Dr Steinberg…is that correct?"

"Yes," I confirm…I'm puzzled as to how they know so much about me, about us, within hours.

"She specializes in grief counselling," I add, feeling a sudden urge to justify and prove we aren't two screwed-up people with a ton of weird issues. Kate is seeing a counsellor for a bone fide reason. As for me, I don't know what the fuck I'm doing…with any of it.

"I'm sorry to hear of your grief Mr Box," Macklin says disingenuously, staring darkly into my eyes. He seems to think he's in 'Silence of the Lambs', this cocky kid… and it takes all my willpower not to lose my cool and take him down a notch.

Will, who has known me forever, can sense my mood darkening and taps my arm lightly as a private signal, letting me know that he will handle this, so I should zip it.

"We won't be needing any of your personal condolences or commentary on each and every answer that my client voluntarily offers, Detective Macklin. Better for everyone that we all stick to facts, as tensions are running high and time is of the essence. I'm sure your boss would agree. Carlisle, isn't it? I know him quite well."

Macklin, for once, doesn't bite back with something sarcastic and seems to adhere to his warning from Will.

I breathe finally. Thank God Will is with me.

"And when exactly did Mr Golding and Mrs Box become aware of the sexual nature of your 'friendship"?" Macklin tilts his head to one side and raises his left eyebrow.

"My wife knows nothing about Kate… but I believe Tom, I mean, Mr Golding, found out about the two of us just this evening. That's why he was here. Did he hurt her? He punched me in the lobby." I point to my swollen eye again. "Did he hurt her too?

I look to Will for answers, but he keeps his face forward and impassive.

Rubbing my eyes roughly with my hands, I try to remember the message that Kate had received and exactly what Tom had said in it.

Macklin exchanges a puzzled glance with the other officer.

"You say your wife knew nothing of the affair, Mr Box? Then can you explain why she was also at the Huxley Hotel this evening?"

CHAPTER 47

HELENA

I had been following them for around nine weeks now. I knew where, I knew when and I knew who.

At first, I had been physically sick with the utter shock and grief. And it was grief. The death of our marriage, the death of our family unit. He's been as vague as can be for as long as I can remember…secretive, defensive and all this time, I thought it was my fault…being too nosey, too needy, too mad.

So many red flags waving frantically before my eyes, but I had never wanted to see what I already knew. The frequent nights away from home and the cold disregard he showed towards me, it should have been enough… but it was his friend, James, who had confirmed things in the end.

Dominic had confided in James, and James confided in his wife, Nicole. It didn't take too much arm-twisting from me for Nicole to admit what she knew. That's the trouble with telling one person; they always tell at least one more. My mother-in-law used to say, "Loose lips, sink ships", and Dominic's lips had caused the Titanic.

I had still hoped it wasn't true. Hoped Nicole had it wrong. Not him? He was a good man underneath his selfish exterior. Except that he wasn't. He was a lying, cheating, weak-willed bastard.

The disappointment was cataclysmic. I couldn't eat, I couldn't sleep, and for reasons I still don't understand, I couldn't confront him either.

Shock, denial, anger, bargaining, depression, testing, acceptance, the seven wonderful stages of grief. I felt each and every one of them until, finally, I felt nothing.

I knew things hadn't been great between us for a long, long time…he didn't see me or value me…I annoyed him by even breathing, and the nicer I became, the more annoyed and distant he became. I even had the GP change my medication. I thought I was mad, and all along, I had been right.

I had to see it with my own eyes. At first, I just occasionally followed him to work before upping my surveillance to his office, his local café, 'The Iris, ' and finally to The Huxley hotel. Always, the same blonde woman would appear just minutes behind him. I soon began to follow her instead.

I wanted to know who she was and quickly became more obsessed with her than with him. I followed her to her local gym and promptly joined myself, watching as she ran, swam and towelled off that perfect body that my husband liked so much. I had never felt hate or jealousy like it, and I tortured myself with thoughts of her daily. The receptionist at the gym told me that her name was Amanda Moretti, and it didn't take much digging to discover that not only was she some kind of filthy escort, but unbelievably she was also his teenage sweetheart from back home. The discovery of that almost killed me right there and then, but still, I didn't confront, and still, I didn't stop following.

The burning anger attached itself to me like a colostomy bag. It followed me, and it followed them. On Thursday night, it followed them to The Huxley hotel for the last time.

CHAPTER 48

TEDDY

Friday

The next morning, I almost forget... just for a second, before the full force of the shit I'm in, smashes into my conscience.

The police detective is back by my bedside and asking more questions regarding my relationship with both Amanda Moretti and Dominic Box. His name is news to me, and I roll the name silently around the inside of my mouth, like a small, unidentifiable marble. The police don't seem too interested in my job or the fraud I have committed, but I very much doubt that means I'm off the hook. They are more interested in any of the other hotel guests that I may have been familiar with and in particular, any friends of Amanda's.

I explain again that Amanda has never mentioned seeing any of her friends at The Huxley, purely that an old friend had recommended the place. They ask if I remember that particular friend's name, but of course, I don't. Right now, I can just about remember my own name.

Amanda, they tell me, has been located and is currently being questioned regarding another incident at the hotel last night. It's hard to keep up, and I'm unsure whether they are referring to the fraud, her blackmailing me, my heavy-handedness with her, the intentions of Jimmy or something entirely different altogether. The Detective remains vague, assuming I know exactly what he is referring to. My head pounds with confusion and fear.

"So, are you familiar with a Mr Dominic Box, Mr Villandry?" The detective perches on the side of the bed, like an over-familiar friend, hoping we might confide in one another over a bunch of grapes.

"Never heard of him," I answer truthfully.

"He's the ex-boyfriend of Amanda Moretti," The Detective says this with slow deliberation and a look that suggests he doesn't believe anything I say.

"Is that Jimmy's real name? Dominic Box? The guy with the moustache?" I'm genuinely confused.

The Detective frowns, confused by my confusion.

"Who's Jimmy?" He asks.

"The guy who was with me when the paramedic arrived. The moustache. He knows Amanda; he was hassling her for money, that's why she...."

"Why she what? What did Ms Moretti do?" He speaks slowly, and I will him to blink, but he's unbreakable.

My guardian angel, Suzie, arrives right on cue and brings the baffling conversation to a temporary close.

"Detective, my husband is still very sick, and these questions will have to wait, I'm afraid".

I smile inwardly at my lovely Suzie, firm but fair, she would have made a fantastic teacher had she ever returned to work, but instead, she had been a wonderful homemaker, raising our children and supporting her jerk of a husband, who was too blind to see the wonderful thing he had in front of him.

She plumps up my pillows and re fills the water jug, bustling around the room, a woman on a mission. The Detective takes the hint, and he and the police officer promise to come back towards the end of the day when I've had more rest.

I close my eyes and listen to the comforting sound of Suzie fussing and tidying my small, private room. Her bracelet jangles like a cat bell as she busies herself with unhelpful but loving nonsense. I want to ask her what's happened to the arsehole? Is he happy with her spending all her free time at my hospital bed? My eyes are heavy, and my mind drifts; I'm too tired to ask.

I finally sink into a deep sleep, but within minutes, I see his baldhead and moustache leaning over me once more, whispering obscenities and threatening to carve up my family. I'm crying out to him, pleading with him not to touch my wife or children. I beg him to kill me and not my family before I remember the letter I wrote.

"What do you need?"

"I need it. I need the letter." I cry

"Teddy? Ted? What letter? What is it?"

I gasp in relief. It's Suzie, not Jimmy. She leans over me and strokes my face as I breathe heavily and clutch at her arms in fear.

"You were having a nightmare, Teddy. Asking for a letter. It must be the drugs they've given to you. Just relax, shhh, now.

She lets herself out of the room to head to the hospital café, and I clutch at my chest. I want this nightmare over.

CHAPTER 49

AMANDA

"No comment", I repeat for the seventh time.

I glance nervously at my lawyer, and he nods his approval.

Liverpool St Police station is possibly the most depressing place I've ever been, and that's saying something.

The grey walls match my mood and are bleak enough to force the most innocent of criminals into a false confession.

My parents had organised a lawyer for me. It was the most hurtful thing about this whole nightmare; they didn't deserve a daughter like me. When the shit kicked in, they were still the only people I could call or count on, and they sent Peter Bannister straight to London to help me. After all these years, I had been looking forward to connecting with them again, showing them how I had turned my life around, how I had fallen in love with their son's best friend again… but now that day would never come. Here I was, back in their lives, with another heap of unimaginable horror at their door.

Peter Bannister was a friend of theirs from way back. I had known him since I was a little girl, although I hadn't seen him since my teens. He was very tall and still had a thick head of hair, although it was now white. He was, as always, immaculately dressed. Peter was very old school and just plain old…but he knew his game and was highly respected in his field, so I trusted him when he insisted I say nothing at all to the police, innocent or not.

When the helicopter had circled above me on The East green, it had near blinded me with the infra-red light, and I had known there was no point in running. There was nowhere to hide. I had never seen anything like it. It was like something from the TV…the amount of police, sirens and now an actual helicopter. I felt terrified and shook with a cold and unknown fright.

I gaze at the grey wall of the interview room as the officer repeats his question for the hundredth time.

I've been here for hours, and we are no further along, thanks to Peter's advice to say nothing.

"Ms Moretti, did you go to the Huxley Hotel this evening with the intention of harming Mrs Golding?"

"No comment" I keep my eyes on the wall and stare at a rogue speck of dirt blotting the blank wall behind the Detective. Dominic must hate me by now, and the thought is excruciating. I don't know how to fix it.

Teddy is alive and in hospital, which I'm relieved about, despite him attacking me last night. I deserved it. I know that. He's a good man. My God, he could have killed himself because of me. Ironic that his drunken body gave way to some kind of stroke before he had the chance. His suicide note is still crumpled up in my handbag. I wonder idly if the police have gone through my bag and read his premature and private farewell. I hope not. I have a feeling he would rather his family didn't ever know of his intention. It's the least I can do for him now.

I wonder if I will ever see Ted again. Doubtful… and the thought fills me with an unexpected sadness.

Nobody seems to be mentioning Jimmy; it's as if he doesn't exist, as if he was never even there in the Hotel.

The memory of him heaving Teddy's unconscious body off my own slides into my head. Jimmy's face had been as purple as Teddy's from the sheer weight of him. As he had turned briefly away from me to roll Teddy back onto the bed, I knew that was my only chance to get out of there. I grabbed my clothes and bag and ran like the wind. The benefit of always folding my clothes into a neat pile, made my getaway possible as I ran naked into the pitch-black corridor from our room.

CHAPTER 50

DOMINIC

"My wife was at the Huxley Hotel???" I look back from Detective Macklin to Will in shock.

"Mrs Box *was* indeed at the Hotel this evening and is now helping us with our enquiries."

"I don't understand" I put my head into my hands. I can't think straight... but really, I do know; of course I know. Any fool would know there could be only one reason that Helena was at the hotel. She knows.

My head is spinning. How long had she known? I try and think back over the past few days and weeks, the conversations we have had, how she has acted around me... or for any obvious signs that she might have known all along. I realise I have barely noticed her in the longest time. She's been tired and extremely quiet, spending her time either lying in front of the TV, staring at the screen blankly or in bed with a book. It annoyed me daily, seeing her laziness, and I had used her lack of energy and conversation as more justification for my lying. To my horror, I realise she knew all along.

"Oh God, did my wife hurt Kate" I sit up suddenly with the realisation.

"DOMINIC" Will shoots me down.

'You don't understand Will…she can be… erratic."

"Excuse me Detective, but my client needs a break to digest this new information," Will tells the Detective firmly.

The Detective nods and signals for his colleague to join him outside.

The door has barely closed before Will wades in; "What the fuck are you doing??? Don't offer them suggestions and SUSPECTS… especially not your own wife. For Christ's sake Dom, think of your kids, man!!"

I can't speak. I'm shaking, and my mind is racing at a thousand miles an hour. I can't take this in. Kate is hurt…seriously hurt. Tom knows about us, and Helena knows too. They were both at the hotel tonight. One of them must have hurt her, and it couldn't be Tom as he was there in the foyer with me. Oh my god, how the fuck am I going to get out of this mess.

Will regains his composure. "Mate, calm down, it's ok. We are going to sort this out. You need to tell me everything. Start from the beginning."

CHAPTER 51

TEDDY

The Detective begins the recording as I prop myself up a little higher on the small hospital bed.

I didn't sleep much last night due to the mental pain ricocheting around my frontal lobe like an angry squash ball. I couldn't get the image of him out of my nightmares. That terrifying face with his twisted moustache and crazed smile.

"Jimmy", she had called him when she began shouting at him. He dragged me off her crushed body, I was falling in and out of consciousness by that point, but I never forget a name.

When I came around…I was propped up in bed, the left side of my face in temporary paralysis, and he was sat watching like a preying bird. Where he had gone since that night, nobody knew. He didn't accompany me to the hospital as he told the medic he would. He just vanished into the night, and nobody seemed interested in why or where, not even the police. He was a person of no interest, yet the most sinister of all.

My belongings from the hotel had been bagged and handed to Suzie to keep for me, and so, as yet, I had not been able to make any calls or check my messages. Not that it would have been wise to try and contact Amanda, but I couldn't help but wonder if she had bothered to check on me… after she fled from my room.

I feel an enormous sense of loss just thinking about her.

"Mr. Villandry. For the benefit of the recording, can you once more confirm your relationship with Amanda Moretti?" The detective interrupts my thoughts

I wince and not from the physical pain. I can barely bring myself to say the words out loud as they sound even sleazier in the cold light of day than I feared.

"I err. I booked Amanda through an escort agency. Bissett's massage agency, off the Edgware Rd." I cough nervously.

"When you say 'escort', can you confirm exactly what that entails?"

I stay silent, staring woefully at my hands.

Mr. Villandry? Was this a sexual relationship? He presses.

"Yes", I admit, sheepishly.

"A sexual relationship that you paid for?"

"Yes." Baaahhs the sheep.

"How well did you know Ms Moretti and her personal life away from your…trysts?" The Detective lingers on the last word to further plough me into the pit of shame.

"We talked quite a lot, believe it or not. Amanda has a few issues, but I have always felt comfortable with her… up until last night."

The detective exchanges glances with his colleague.

"What happened last night that left you feeling 'uncomfortable' around Ms Moretti?"

"She was blackmailing me," I say, feeling like I'm in an episode of Dynasty. How can this be my actual life? I'm just a normal, everyday guy, and yet somehow, I'm here in this madness.

"Blackmailing you about what? Did she threaten to tell Mrs Villandry that you were paying her for sex?"

I wince again.

"Noooo, no. It's nothing like that. Nothing to do with Suzie; she doesn't know any of it, and we are separated anyway. Amanda was blackmailing me for money. I didn't realise it was her sending the e-mails… until last night."

"If she wasn't threatening to tell your wife about the paid sex, then what else did she have on you?" The Detective purses his lips with a look of boredom.

"It's complicated. It's connected to my work. I got fired yesterday for…err… misconduct' I feel the shiftiness shadow my face as I settle on the ambiguous word.

" Amanda knew about it…and had been threatening to tell my boss…unless I paid a ridiculous amount of money into an unknown account that she had set up".

"Was Ms Moretti openly blackmailing you about this?"

"No…like I said, she had set up a fake account and was emailing me anonymously. I had no idea it was her…not until last night."

"You say you got fired yesterday? So, presumably, Ms Moretti carried out her threat and informed your boss? The Detective scratches his stubbly chin, a habit he repeats throughout and which, for some reason, I keep fixating on to stop me from completely losing my mind with this blind car crash.

"I don't know. No…I don't think so, actually?" I'm pretty sure it didn't play out that way in the end. "Charles, my boss said that they had found a couple of emails between the blackmailer and I after becoming worried about my state of mind at work and having them checked. I like to think she wouldn't have gone through with it, but maybe that's wishful thinking. I wasn't going to hurt her, not really" I cover my face with my hands and embarrassingly start to cry.

The Detective looks uncomfortable with my tears. His alpha chest expands in disgust at my unmanly display.

"Is it possible that Amanda Moretti was also blackmailing Kate Golding?"

I scrunch my face in confusion.

"I honestly have no idea who this woman is, and Amanda has never mentioned her. There is no connection between her and the attack on the other guest" I shake my head with certainty.

"Amanda Moretti is the ex-girlfriend of Kate Golding's lover. Mrs Golding is currently in intensive care, and I have CCTV footage of Amanda Moretti heading up to Mrs Golding's Suite at around the time of the attack. It's grainy due to the lack of light, but her distinctive hair confirms it's her. I would say that's a pretty strong connection, Ted".

JASON

"I'm pumped up with adrenalin as I helpfully talk Detective Macklin through his 'enquiries'. The filth needs MY help, and it feels good.

"You say you have seen Kate Golding and Dominic Box fairly regularly at the Huxley Hotel for over a year now? Is that right, Jason?"

"Regular as clockwork, mate. Every Thursday, up to no good," I chortle and look around, grinning broadly at my audience. The Detective and two other police officers eyeball me with suspicion. Three little pigs trying to blow my house down.

"What is the relationship between Mrs Golding, Mr Box and the other regular guests, Mr Villandry and Ms Moretti? Do they come to The Huxley together as a four? Do they socialise together?

"I think he's knocking the pair of them off, lucky bastard," I added, warming to my crowd.

"Who? Mr Box?" The Detective asks

"Yeah…I've seen him with both birds, for sure. He clearly has a type. Have you seen them? They look fairly alike." I lean back and let out a yawn. It's been a long night and an even longer morning. As much as I'm enjoying the buzz, I'm getting hungry, bored and a bit pissed off now.

"You seem to have paid an extraordinary amount of attention to the guests at the hotel…wouldn't you say, Jason?"

I don't care for this mush's tone, and I stare him down

"That's what I'm paid to do, innit."

"Are you also paid to make handwritten notes about the movements of individual guests? What they eat, what they drink, what they wear? Not to mention your own little character assassination on each guest." He waves my grubby notebook in the air in his left hand.

How the fuck has he found that?

"That's private," I yell, attempting to snatch it out of his hand.

"Something to hide in here, Jason. If not, you won't mind us finishing your little story, as personally, I can't wait to see what happens at the end."

I rock back on my chair again, just to piss him off. PIG."

CHAPTER 52

AMANDA

"I didn't attack her," I say for the first time.

The Detective sits up straight.

Peter shoots a look to quieten me down, but I'm tired of this. We're going around in circles, and it's like Chinese torture. I've been here all night and all day, and this 'no comment' strategy of Pete's is getting me absolutely nowhere. They have no intention of letting me go, and I feel like I'm going mad in here.

"I think that's the smartest decision you have made so far, Ms Moretti. We are indeed getting nowhere with this 'no comment' game, so let's start talking."

"Can you confirm the reason for your stay at The Huxley Hotel on the evening of Thursday, November the seventh?"

‘I was meeting Ted Villandry for the evening,” I tell him.

“Was it your intention to spend the whole night at the hotel?”

“Yes. I don’t often stay the whole night, but I stayed over last Friday and had intended to stay again this evening. Teddy arranged it. Obviously, that didn’t happen.”

“How well do you know Mr Villandry?”

“I’ve been meeting him at The Huxley a couple of times a week for the past four or five months,” I say, shooting Peter a look to warn him off interrupting me. He sighs and puts his fancy pen down on top of his file.

“What was the relationship between yourself and Mr Villandry?”

“He booked me. I’m an escort. Teddy is a regular client of mine and a decent guy.” I’m brazen and defiant despite my fear.

“Escorting might lead us to believe that you were simply a companion of Mr Villandry’s. Is it more accurate to say that Mr Villandry was, in fact, booking you as a prostitute for a sexual transaction? Not simply ‘escorting’?”

“Yes,” I confirm.

Neither the Detective nor I miss the sudden disappearance of Peter’s white eyebrows, but he remains stoic and silent.

"So, Mr Villandry had booked you through the agency for the entire night, and you say that this was a little unusual?"

"I didn't say it was unusual. Teddy often paid me for the entire night even though I didn't often stay over. The agency said he was insistent that I should be free to stay last night and not have anyone else booked in. He obviously needed the company."

"Would it be fair to say that Teddy had been in a state of distress more recently, and this could perhaps explain his "need" for company, as you put it?"

"I wouldn't say he's been distressed. I guess a little preoccupied with work, life, you know, the usual's…."

"Is it usual in your line of work to be blackmailed then, Ms Moretti?"

I blush but don't answer as Peter shoots a look of confusion at both the Detective and I, as if he has perhaps misheard the last part.

"Can you confirm your relationship with Mrs Golding?"

"Mrs Golding? Kate? I err; I have no relationship with her. I met her briefly, once for a few minutes, in the bar. She was in a relationship with an old friend of mine" My heart starts to race a little quicker, and the back of my knees feel slick with cold sweat.

'I think 'old friend' is perhaps doing a disservice to your relationship with Mr Box, wouldn't you say?'

'I hadn't seen Dominic Box for many years until recently." I'm faltering

'You have an obsession with Mr Box. Wouldn't that be more accurate?'

"Don't be ridiculous", I shoot. "He was an ex-boyfriend from a billion years ago. I hadn't seen him for at least fifteen years until I bumped into him randomly a few weeks ago at The Huxley.'

"There was nothing random about your re-acquaintance with Mr Box; was there Ms Moretti? Neither was there anything random in your choice of hotel, and there was certainly nothing random in CCTV picking up your black BMW, parked outside Mr Box's home, his work and his counsellor's office on several occasions. Your browser history certainly makes for an interesting read".

"NO COMMENT," I say.

"Let's not be silly, Ms Moretti. If you are innocent, then you will have no problem answering a few difficult questions in order for us to eliminate you from our enquiries.

"Can you confirm for the recording that this knife belongs to you, Ms Moretti?"

I recoil as he lays a picture flat on the table in front of me. My bread knife, the one I use every day at home, with its scuffed wooden handle, is photographed there in plain sight.

"Would you like some water, Ms Moretti?" The detective clicks his fingers at the police officer, who disappears like smoke.

"Yes… it's my knife," I whisper.

"I would like to take a break with my client, Detective Macklin?" Peter interrupts. He can't hold it in any longer and is horrified at my candid talk and dubious lifestyle, but I can't sit here any longer; I'm getting absolutely nowhere, and my head is about to burst.

"NO." I slam my palm, flat onto the table.

"Yes. That is my knife…my rusty, innocuous bread knife. I use it at home every single day to slice bread'. The sarcasm does nothing to hide my panic and rising voice.

"Would you care to explain why it is that you should be carrying this 'innocuous' and innocent bread knife from your home and into a hotel, where you were due to meet Mr Villandry? Where you and Mr Villandry planning on making sandwiches, perhaps?"

The second police officer lets out a small laugh, but the detective quietens him with a hard stare.

I don't answer.

"Did you go to the Huxley Hotel with the intention of harming Mrs Golding?"

I don't answer.

"Is it true that you were driven mad with jealousy over her relationship with your ex-lover, Mr Box?"

"NOOOOO. You've got it all wrong. Yes, I was a little jealous, but I wouldn't attack anyone. I wouldn't hurt anyone. I didn't."

I wonder fleetingly where Jimmy is. Nobody seems to be mentioning him. It's as if he was never there when all of this is because of HIM. This is entirely his fault, every single part of it.

The blackmailing of Teddy happened so that I could pay Jimmy back. Carrying the knife was to protect myself from Jimmy's threats. Teddy is laid up in hospital, a suspected stroke brought on from the stress of my blackmail, no doubt. I would never have the knife in my bag in the first place if it were not for Jimmy and his endless threats.

"You must realise that being armed with a weapon suggests exactly that intention, Ms Moretti?"

"No comment," barks Peter.

JASON

"You mention in your little journal something about a man with a bald head and moustache, whom you claim to have spotted in close proximity to Mr Villandry and Ms Moretti's room on the fourth floor? Is that correct, Jason?" The detective taps his finger onto the open page of the notepad, and Jason notices the old brown stain of ketchup smeared across his handwriting.

"Yep, that's right. Shifty-looking bloke and a friend of Ted Villandry." He smirks, enjoying how much they need his info.

"We have no such sighting of anyone matching that description on the CCTV, Jason?"

"That's because the cameras were switched off," Jason smirks without thinking.

"And why would that be? Who switched the camera's off?"

"Err, Steve…the other security guard. He's new and a bit wide, I think. He was often switching them off so that he could have a wander around the hotel…you know, along the stairwell. Nosey bastard he is." He coughs as the Detective eyeballs him silently.

Maybe he would look into training as a copper himself when all this is over, Jason thought to himself. He idly wondered how much they must earn. A hell of a lot more than he made working security at that knocking shop.

"So, you know this as fact, do you, Jason? The guy with the moustache and Mr Villandry are friends?"

"Well, I presume so; this mush has been following him around enough times recently."

"How about you don't 'presume' anything, Jason? You leave the presumptions to the police and stick to hard facts."

"Yes sir", He mocks, with a little salute as he tips back on the hind legs of his chair and rocks gently." He's dying for a smoke, but they have already vetoed that, the bloody fun police. He laughs out loud at his own joke."

CHAPTER 53

HELENA

I had sat in the far corner of the Hux restaurant on the ground floor of the hotel. They couldn't see me, but I could see them…both of them. He didn't take his lying eyes off her, even for a second, and my heart ached.

I watched as she stuffed her face with bread, smearing it with butter, not a care in the world.

I stared at the back of her blonde head. This woman.

Amanda Moretti had taken my husband and my life from right under my nose. What did she have that I didn't? What did she have that he wanted so much? So much that he would wreck his entire family for her.

She was pretty, no doubt. Beautiful. I had gazed at her enough times in her gym. The blonde hair, the plump mouth and the fancy clothes. All so obvious, but he had fallen hook, line and sinker for this walking cliché. She clearly had not a care in the world. The kind of woman who has it all but still wants more regardless. This modern-day Jolene sitting with my husband.

I sipped on the sparkling water that the waiter had shamed me into ordering whilst I waited longer than he liked for my imaginary 'friend'.

I had decided that tonight I would finally confront the pair of them.

I had spent the week rummaging through his desk at home, looking at receipt after receipt from their clandestine dinners, hotels, cinema trips, coffees and even tickets to a gallery in Mayfair. This wasn't just sex or lust; this was a full-blown love affair, and the realisation punched me deep down in my gut. My heart rattled with it all, and my head raged. I had spent two hours cross-referencing the dates of his receipts against the dates that he had been away with work or out with 'James'. Most of the dates matched perfectly. Liar, liar, LIAR.

He had crucified me over the years, encouraged me not to work then grown bored of me when I had nothing to talk about other than the kids. He had talked over me, ignored me, belittled me, cheated endlessly, lied and denied and then blamed it all on me for being mad, menopausal, paranoid or needy. I had taken it, day and day, year after year, and now he planned to just throw me out with the trash and walk away with a new model.

Over my dead body…or hers.

I sipped my water and watched as he paid the bill in the restaurant for his fancy woman out of our family money. I wanted to throw up right there on the table with its beautiful white linen tablecloth. The two of them stood to leave, and I watched his hand on her arse as he led her out of the restaurant towards the lift. The bile rose like fire in my throat as I slugged back the rest of my water. I had no choice but to follow them up to their room.

CHAPTER 54

TOM

"Did you know of Amanda Moretti before receiving the letter informing you of your wife's affair? Detective Carlisle sits forward on the hospital chair, one elbow on each knee, legs wide. He looked like a rugby player, not a cop.

"I've never heard of her. The letter was anonymous, so I was not aware who sent it until you told me," I reply.

I hold my head in my hands as I perch on the edge of the worn, pale pink sofa in the inappropriately cheery and floral waiting room, next to the ICU at St Leonards hospital.

"Detective Carlisle. Mr Golding has just suffered an enormous shock and should be allowed to sit with his wife. I am sure these questions can wait until tomorrow." The Doctor cuts in, leaving the Detective open-mouthed, poised with his next question, which hangs in mid-air.

"I'm afraid such questions cannot wait, Dr Wilton…as you are aware, this is an attempted murder investigation, and therefore the immediate hours following such an event are absolutely crucial to this case. Now… we can continue at the station, but one presumes it would be more comfortable for Mr Golding to stay here, under these difficult circumstances." The Detective is gentle but firm, leaving both Dr Wilson and I in no doubt, that questions will indeed be answered.

"Who do you think tried to kill Kate?" I say.

My voice cracks at the mention of her name, and my mind fills with thoughts of Freddie. His Mother is breathing, but as yet, they can't confirm if she has suffered any brain damage. I can't break his heart and tiny little world all over again for the second time in his short life.

"Mrs Box is currently answering questions at Liverpool Street station, as is Ms Moretti and as soon as we have any further information, you will be the first to know, Mr Golding. Tell me though; I'm interested to know… what made you believe an anonymous stranger?' The Detective looks faintly amused, as if waiting for a humorous anecdote to unfold.

"Just a feeling," I tell him.

Carlisle slaps his hands on his thighs.

"Then you must be a clairvoyant Mr Golding… such strong feelings led you to the exact hotel on the exact night, and I don't believe that was mentioned in Ms Moretti's letter to you. Tell me, were these feelings confirmed only after you had broken into your wife's office?" Carlisle rubs his stubbled jaw as he ponders.

"I didn't break in. I had the key." I tell him.

"Aaahhh, my misunderstanding.

Well, perhaps you can confirm your whereabouts last night? Only… your altercation with Mr Box was around nine pm, yet you are seen arriving in the hotel foyer around six forty-five. Were you sat in the reception with these funny feelings of yours for over two hours prior?

The Detective sounds a little less gentle this time, and I notice Dr Wilson flashing a look of disgust his way.

Carlisle smiles gently at the Doctor, triumph proudly gleaming from his slanted eyes.

"Please leave." Commands Dr Wilton, flashing him a withering look despite her uncertainty over my dubious answers.

"Mr Golding, it appears we will need to take you down to the station after all."

CHAPTER 55

DOMINIC

Kate could be dead by now, for all I knew. I was not afforded the right to further information on her. I wasn't her husband, her next of kin or her family. I was nothing. In an instant, it's all reduced to a great dirty nothingness as I sit in this grey, soulless interview room.

Kate and I are nothing more than a grubby shag to the disparaging police officers as they colour by numbers with their distorted picture of two horrible narcissists, meeting purely for sex in a seedy hotel room. Rage bubbles under the surface of my skin as I listen to their snide remarks and sarcastic questions, all fired at me with intent, as they presume to know everything about us.

I wanted to stand up and smash the table, to shout and tell these fuckers they were wrong.

The Detective's voice violently interrupts my rising distress as he reloads his gun. I breathe in and sit up a little taller, ready for his next cheap shot.

"You didn't think it strange at all then? That Ms Moretti, your former girlfriend, was also a regular guest at the same hotel? The same hotel that you and Mrs Golding frequented week after week on the same day? Perhaps you had arranged this set-up yourself with Ms Moretti?"

"WHAT set up?? There was no set-up?" I bawl.

"Had Ms Moretti and Mrs Golding had any previous altercation that you were aware of, before last night Mr Box?"

"What are you talking about?" I bang my fist on the table in frustration. "They don't even know each other; they met only once and briefly at that. There was and is no altercation. Why would there be??"

The Detective allows a blanket of silence to envelope us for much longer than is comfortable before he warms once more to his theme and fires at point-blank range.

"Ms Moretti is currently being questioned over the murder of Mrs Golding. Amanda Moretti had been following the two of you for several months, and evidence to confirm this is scattered all over her flat. There are pictures of you with Mrs Golding, pictures of your wife, and dates and times of your regular whereabouts and not just at the hotel. Were you or were you not aware that Ms Moretti intended to harm Mrs Golding?"

I turn, open-mouthed to Will, who remains impassive. I can't comprehend what I'm hearing. Mimi had been following us. Whaaaat? This was utter madness.

"No comment," Will says firmly.

JASON

"You spoke to Amanda Moretti in the stairwell this evening? Are you sure about that, Jason?" The Detective repeats himself, disbelief furrowing along his brow.

"Yep, that's what I said. I was standing at the bottom, having a butcher's through the door to the reception; it was all kicking off. Somebody came into the stairwell but then scarpered back up. I can't be too sure who, as it was pitch black.

I carried on watching the fight in reception but then heard somebody else coming into the stairwell. This time I got a proper look, and it was Teddy Villandry's tart. She fell…pretty much at my damn feet. Jason laughed.

"The mad bitch was racing down the stairs, which was stupid in the dark, especially if you don't know the stairwell as I do. Her bag spilt crap out everywhere, and the slapper only had a knife on her too!" Jason's eyes light up at his new revelation.

"Yep, it came flying out of her handbag, no word of a lie, then the stupid cow fell and cracked her head. Jason rocks back in his seat."

'I reckon it must have been her that drowned the other poor bird. Catfight gone wrong; that's my guess. You know what these bitches are like. Savage.'

"We won't be needing you to make any wild guesses; thank you, Jason."

"The two blondes are never usually here on the same night, up until recently, that is. I never seen that third woman before though?" Jason points at the picture of Helena Box. He rocks back and forward again until the Detective snaps at him to stop. What's with this prick?

The Detective replaces the picture with one of that stuck-up whore instead.

"Jason, can you confirm that the woman you saw in the stairwell was absolutely Ms Amanda Moretti, seen here in the image shown?"

"Oh yeah, that's her alright. Stuck up bitch she is. You know she's a prozzie as well? Miss High and Mighty. She was still mouthing off at me, even when I helped her out of the back door. Ungrateful bitch. I had her filthy blood all over me from her fall."

CHAPTER 56

HELENA

I followed them up to the third floor and sat cross-legged and bereft on the carpeted floor outside their room. I listened to the painful sound of moaning and laughing that came faintly from within. The corridor was pitch black for some reason, but it suited me fine as I sat frozen for what seemed like days. I had wanted so much to confront them, to hurt them as much as they were hurting me… but hearing them; I had felt rigid and strangely calm. I stayed still.

I'm not sure I would have ever moved had it not been for the arrival of the bellboy bringing their ice-cold champagne and silver dishes full of fancy food. It looked like a celebration, a feast with no expense spared.

When was the last time he had taken me away for a night…anywhere? The last time he had excitedly ordered cold champagne and expensive food? My heart ached with sadness and loss. I could be as angry as I liked, but I could never change the fact that he was in love with someone else.

I sat still in the shadows.

CHAPTER 57

AMANDA

Kate had been drowned and left almost for dead. Found floating naked in the same clear tank that Teddy and I had slipped in and out of, week after week, at The Duke of Shoreditch Suite.

The bellboy had dragged her out after noticing the door was wide open. He had pumped a ton of water out of her and resuscitated her just enough before the ambulance arrived. Now they were monitoring her for secondary drowning at St Leonard's hospital, and by all accounts, it didn't look good.

The Detective's voice drones on and on as his faint words spin around like dirty laundry in a washing machine, along with the other distorted thoughts in my brain.

I hear him ask if the knife found by a security guard at the hotel was 'my' knife. Had I taken it to the hotel with the intention of hurting Kate Golding?

"Helena Box," I say calmly.

"Excuse me?" Says the Detective.

"I saw Dominic Box's wife leaving the Duke of Shoreditch Suite…maybe she tried to drown Kate for sleeping with her husband… then came to her senses?." I put my head into my hands.

I wanted to throw up…I may as well have killed her myself.

I had led Helena directly to Kate. I had made sure they were caught. I had proved to Helena that she was right all along about Dominic's cheating… and now Kate was lying in a coma.

CHAPTER 58

TEDDY

Detective Carlisle looks unusually cheery as he bounds into my hospital room and perches himself back on the end of the bed like an old, familiar friend.

He looks rather groomed, I note. His shirt has seen an actual iron, and he appears fresh and well-rested, which is a first.

"Good news" he clasps his hands together like a priest about to deliver mass and turn my water into wine. His holy demeanour is particularly at odds with his rugged face, and that dislocated big nose of his. He immediately unsettles me.

“Helena Box has been charged with the murder of Mrs Katherine Golding.’ He opens his arms wide, awaiting gasps from his congregation.

“Who?” I didn’t know these Box people he kept speaking of, but I had known all along that Amanda had been innocent. She may have been capable of many things, but she was certainly not a murderer. Though why she had been carrying a knife, Lord only knew. It must have been because of Jimmy, blackmailing her… just as she had blackmailed me.

“Ms Moretti still has questions to answer regarding her possession of a weapon. Not to mention the level of stalking and sightings around Mr Box and Mrs Golding…but wait for the best news Teddy.” He smacks my leg hard to labour his point. “We also have enough evidence to charge her with twelve counts of blackmail against you.’ He beams at me as if I have just won a top-of-the-range Ford Galaxy and a timeshare in The Algarve.

I think he is waiting for some kind of gushing thank you, some showy level of gratitude, but I’m numb and disorientated.

“I won’t be pressing charges against her,” I bleat. ‘I know her. She’s a good person.”

“That may not be your choice, Mr Villandry. She will have a hard time convincing any jury that she is as good a person as you claim. She is a prostitute who came to the hotel in possession of a knife, having stalked her ex-lover for months. She also blackmailed you for an extraordinary amount of money. Your loyalty to her is admirable. She must be excellent at her job." He raises his brow and smirks.

Carlisle stands up from the bed and is about to turn when he makes a theatrical show of remembering something else. He waves one finger in the air, turns back toward me and leans in closer with this sudden afterthought.

"Oh, before I forget, once you're up and about again, we can have a chat about all this money laundering nonsense. You never know, you may end up meeting Mrs Box... when you're in the same nick."

He smacks my leg one more time with a beaming grin.

I'm silently crying again, I don't know what's wrong with me, but I'm so traumatised that I don't notice Suzie sitting in the corner, listening to everything… not until Detective Carlisle leaves and bids her good day.

My face is as white as a sheet as I look to her for pardon. My eyes search hers to read her thoughts. She knows who Amanda is; it's written all over her face.

"Suzie", I start…

"Sebastian and Lucinda told me what was going on at work a short time ago before you were fired.

"You know about the money?" I whisper

"I thought I knew about everything, Teddy…until now".

I gasp and search her pretty face for any hint of emotion, but she is blank.

"How could you? A prostitute? Dear god, Teddy… how could you do this to the kids?

I try and prop my body up a little higher on the hospital pillow.

"Nooooo, Suzie, it wasn't like that." I'm crying, but she quietens me with her sensible teacher's voice.

'Teddy, you are probably going to prison, and you're certainly never going to work again, other than packing shelves. I could kill you myself for what you've done to this family… but I will protect you as much as I can for the sake of the children. She wipes away her tears on the back of her sleeve.

"Suzie, I'm so sorry" I break into huge, racking sobs, shame filling my lungs. "I love you, Suzie; I'm so sorry."

"I love you too," She whispers. "We'll be ok" She squeezes my hand tight.

CHAPTER 59

HELENA

After the bellboy had delivered their feast and cold champagne, I had sat still for what felt like hours but must have been only around ten minutes.

It was only the pitch black that saved Amanda Moretti from seeing me when she burst unexpectedly from the suite she shared with my husband. Except it wasn't Amanda Moretti. I know that now. His mistress was never Amanda Moretti; his mistress was Kate Golding.

Kate Golding was a married mother of two, with one child deceased. She was thirty- eight and ran her own small Company. She had her own husband who loved her, and she also had my husband who loved her. Kate Golding was now fighting for her life.

I had held my breath when Dominic, minutes later, had emerged, dressed and hurrying toward the lift.

He didn't see me, he never saw me anymore, but I could certainly see him.

The lack of light in the corridor had kept me hidden. He had left the door to their room ajar, but my body remained rigid. I couldn't bear to get up and look inside at their filth.

I sat still, barely breathing.

The last thing I expected to see was Kate scurrying back towards their room minutes later and disappearing back inside.

The Detective tells me that I have killed her. He tells me that I tried to drown Kate Golding in a fit of rage or a 'crime passional,' as he refers to it. He tells me that I have been seen following her and my husband to The Huxley for several weeks; he also tells me that I was seen on CCTV outside their room and that Amanda Moretti has also placed me outside their room at that exact time.

I wanted to kill her. It was true…but I had been too cowardly. Instead, I sat frozen. So frozen that I hadn't reacted at all, not to any of it. I hadn't reacted to their moaning and lovemaking nor their laughter; I hadn't reacted to the arrival of room service or even to their lover's tiff. So frozen that I hadn't even reacted to the shadowy figure that had followed Kate back into their suite. I had presumed it was Dominic

Instead, I walked away. I had seen enough. I wanted to go home. I walked away from the room. When I finally looked up, I gasped …the other woman, the woman I had been following… Amanda Moretti was standing in front of me by the fire escape door. How could she be here and yet inside the suite? I was confused. My God, was he sleeping with two women? I wailed in pure pain, before running…running away from the whole mess.

Behind me, I heard Amanda Moretti rushing towards the suite, bashing on the door and calling out my husband's name.

JASON

"The detective tells Jason that, for now, he is no longer needed with their enquiries. He also informs him that he's been fired from the Huxley Hotel.

"Fired for what?" Jason yelled as The Detective tried to usher him out of the interview room and on his way.

"Where would you like me to start, Jason?" Detective Macklin waved his hand towards the door to signal his time was up.

Jason stormed past him, eyeballing the cunt on his way out.

Had he known he was going to be sacked anyway, he might have been a little more helpful from the start. Had they played nice, he might have mentioned his hidden camera. Finally, he had planted it inside The Duke of Shoreditch suite just last week… after sharing a smoke with those dopey cleaners.

He hadn't had time to watch last night's show yet and was buzzing from the possibilities he may find, after what had gone down at the Hotel.

He called in at the one-stop shop on his way home from the police station, treating himself to a frozen pizza and a large bottle of cider with the twenty quid note he had nicked from Steve's drawer.

Time to watch the final episode.

Jason rigged up his laptop and sat back on the damp old sofa, taking a greedy bite of his limp pepperoni pizza.

The Duke of Shoreditch suite came into view on his screen for the very last time.

He unbuckled his belt and let out a long groan as he enjoyed the live sex show between the bath woman and Dominic Box. Christ, this was better than a lot of the porn hub he watched. A proper snuff movie.

They were going for it as well. Jason fast-forwarded through their boring chitchat and through the arrival of the bellboy with more food and plonk.

He pressed fast-forward again with a bored sigh as he saw the blonde bird leaving the room, followed by Box, chasing after her. The recording ran a little too far ahead, and he saw two grainy figures coming back into the room. Jason re-wound a little and sat back down.

The blonde woman came back into the suite. She sat herself on the bed, leaning forward with her head in her hands. Jason took another swig of cider, choking slightly as he saw her begin to undress. "Oh, here we go, yes!" he shouted at the screen, leaning forward to get another close-up of her naked body. The bitch was going to have a dip in the tank, stark bollock naked.

He gazed at her face, her tits and her lovely legs, sculling in the water of the clear tank. She turned her back to the camera and let her face fall forward onto her bent forearms at the edge of the tank. Her long blonde hair grazed the middle of her back as she kicked her legs out behind her to stay afloat. Lovely Jason was admiring the sight of her ass when he suddenly slammed down his cider on the table.

"FUCK" he shouted loudly, hitting pause on the screen. He rewound again slightly and zoomed in on the large hand that had appeared at the back of her neck. That was no woman's hand. Those were not Helena Box's hands.

Jason pressed play and, open-mouthed, zoomed in on the clear image of that bloke with the twisted moustache. Pushing her blonde head under the water, he didn't let go until her beautiful legs kicked no more.

CHAPTER 60

FIVE MONTHS LATER:

Teddy

I pour myself a nice, real coffee and grin at Suzie as she hands me a doorstep slice of her banana bread and kisses my cheek.

I'm exhausted...another day of community service, collecting stinking rubbish from the streets and today's highlight, scrubbing away a giant neon dick that had been spray painted onto the bakery window on the Elmswood estate.

Dick or no dick...I feel happier than I've felt in months.

I would never be employed in my sector again; I would repay every last penny, tricky on the admin job Seb had, tricky on the admin job, Seb had promised, but it didn't matter. I had Suzie. I had my family back. I was alive.

KATE

"Jules, can you get that…I think it's Tom and Freddie."

I hear Jules welcoming Tom into his old home and talking nine to the dozen to fill in any awkward silence.

Tom sounds polite, uncertain of his place in our new world and hovers in our hallway.

"Come in", I call from the kitchen. 'Jules has made lasagne, and there's enough to feed an army…stay and eat?"

He nods gratefully and smiles without teeth. We are nervous and delicate but kind.

It had taken weeks to recover, and I still didn't feel back to full strength, but I was alive and glad to be so.

"Hey darling", I squeeze Freddie into a tight hug, sniffing his hair and breathing in every inch of him. We've agreed alternate weekends and every Wednesday night for now, and Freddie has settled in fairly easily those nights at Tom's flat. Things are as amicable as possible, which is nothing short of a miracle, considering.

Tom had been prepared to forgive me. Forgive the affair, the lies and the horror of that night, and it would have been easier to stay and grab onto that forgiveness with two hands, to thank God that I had been given another chance. But deep down, I knew it was *me* that couldn't fully forgive Tom. Logically I knew it wasn't his fault; I knew he was crucified by losing Connie too…but I also knew that we would both hold onto our resentments forever more if we didn't break away and heal separately.

Dominick had never once tried to contact me after that night. Like a fool, I had messaged and called…at first demanding to know why he hadn't even bothered to check I was alive…then pleading and apologising for what? I didn't even know…only that I felt desperate and unable to accept even more loss.

Without the distraction of Dominick, I would surely feel the absence of Connie even more acutely.

Finally, after five long months, I had messaged him to say goodbye…an acceptance of all that had passed between us and all that would now never be. It was the only message he bothered to reply to.

'Sure, take care.'

His careless flippancy was as crushing as his silence had been.

Jules had moved in just for two weeks… (around four months ago) just as Tom had moved out, and actually, we had grown fond of having each other around. It had been better for Freddie to have a little more life-breathing through the house, and her endless dating stories took my mind off things each night.

Tom and I were finally reaching a better place, Freddie was doing ok, and The Pink Pig was busier than ever. For now, it was all I could hope for. Peace.

Dominick

I slammed the door as the third lot of viewers trundled off down the drive with that arrogant prick from the estate agents.

The nerve of him, quietly asking that I not be in my own house next time as apparently I was putting potential buyers off with my 'aura'.

I bet the prick didn't even know what aura was… he must have been twenty-one if he was a day.

When Helena had first been held in custody for the attempted manslaughter of Kate, it was impossible to comprehend on any possible level and had shaken us to the core. The humiliation and embarrassment of having every Tom, Dick and Harry knowing our business were worse than the event itself.

Will, as a favour to me, had been working around the clock as her lawyer to help our family out of this nightmare.

So it was a kick in the teeth that Helena had immediately begun divorce proceedings while still in custody, and it looked like the bitch was going to take me to the cleaners.

I felt furious all day and all night at the moment; how dare she snoop around on me, pretending not to know all of this time, checking up on me for god knows how long and now bringing all this public shame to our door. People had affairs every day…*their* wives didn't try and kill anyone. She was mad…absolutely mad.

The news was all over the kids' school and had been exaggerated wildly, which caused them all kinds of distress. Needless to say, they had refused to go to school for weeks on end, meaning I couldn't go to work, and that gave my boss the perfect excuse to make me quietly redundant and distance the company from all this stink.

I grab another beer and lay back on the sofa, staring at the TV despite it being off. I need to look for a job and a smaller place, but I'm too angry to even search.

I scroll through my phone and look at the endless messages from Kate over these past few months…

pleading, apologising, declaring love. I had wanted to distance myself as far away as possible from her and this chaos and had closed her down several months ago.

Although in hindsight…It would have been better to keep things going with her; maybe I could move into her place for a while.

I type out a quick message…

'Hello Mrs Wilding…been thinking about you. D x'

JASON

"They hadn't been able to give me my job back, due to me filming inside the rooms and all… but in the end, I had made more money than I ever would have done staying in that shitty hotel.

I had only handed the recording over to prove to the filth that I wasn't the useless mug they thought I was. I couldn't have cared less really about Helena Box and certainly didn't want to do her husband any favours. But everyone acted like I was Mother Theresa when Mrs Box was let off with the charges, thanks to my evidence… and the hunt had begun for the weirdo with the tache.

Joseph had brought my last paycheck to the flat in person and patted my back as he left like I was one of his important hotel guests. Even Steve had bobbed around to the flat and brought me a Kit Kat. The best part, however, was the interview I did for the Sunday Mirror, where they asked all kinds of details about

Box and who he had been shagging. I had plenty to say on that, and they handed me enough money to retire for the next few years. Justice at last."

AMANDA

"Ms Moretti", gasps Joseph the maître d…his shock at seeing me back at The Huxley is etched clearly across his shiny, tanned brow.

"Hello, Joseph."

"How are you, Ms Moretti?"

"I've been better, Joseph," I say, putting it mildly

"I'm so very sorry for what happened … here at the hotel." He looks genuinely saddened.

"Thank you, Joseph." I tap his arm lightly, a gesture of goodwill.

"I'm not staying here …obviously. I just wanted to come for a drink in the bar, if that's still ok?" I'm hesitant and unsure of myself. It's a new me, a broken me.

"Of course, Ms Moretti. Head on through to the lounge bar and tell Rico that your first drink is on the house." He returns the arm pat and tips his head at me, an old-fashioned but terribly sweet gesture.

I sit myself at the bar and gaze into the bottom of my sparkling water. I can feel Dominic and Teddy all around the place. I can see them. I can hear Teddy and I laughing, and I can smell our memories mixed in with the familiar scent of the room. It's amazing how a smell can transport you right back in time, to a place and to a person. I breathe it in, wanting to feel closer to both of them again.

I was partly to blame for ruining Dominic's life, and understandably he wanted nothing to do with me, for now at least.

He had to leave his job to take care of the kids when Helena was initially in custody, and then on her release, when she had suffered a complete breakdown and gone to her parents for 6 months.

Kate was back home, working again, taking care of her son and separated from Tom, according to the local papers.

Teddy hadn't returned any of my early calls those first few weeks, and now I knew Suzie had taken him back, I understood why. I'm happy for him; if anyone deserved a second chance, it was Teddy.

I left Bissett's agency, got myself a normal job in retail and quit my reflexology course. I've moved to a different part of London and changed my number once again. Time for a fresh start.

I just needed to come back here, one last time and say goodbye. Some kind of closure.

I have no right to self-pity; that was purely the right of Tom and Freddie Golding. They were the innocent people in all of this. I had no right to feel sorry for myself, although, of course, I did.

I wave my hand at Rico and make the universal sign for the bill. I don't deserve a free drink. I glance at my phone, and my skin goes cold. I look quickly over my shoulder and around the whole of the bar, hunting for him, eyeing each and every guest, searching for his twisted moustache… before looking back to the message again.

WhatsApp

"Hello Mandy. Looks like I got the wrong girl…."

THE END